A LANTERN IN THE WINDOW

Bobby Hutchinson

A LANTERN IN THE WINDOW
© Copyright 2011 Bobby Hutchinson
ALL RIGHTS RESERVED

For my mother, Bertha Dahl Rothel, whose vivid memories of those pioneer times inspire many of my stories. Thanks for the memories, Mom.

Chapter One

February 22, 1886

"She's good and late. Prob'ly hit a blizzard."

The garrulous man also awaiting the arrival of the westbound train tugged his knitted cap closer around his ears and huddled into his woolen overcoat, eyeing Noah's heavy buffalo coat with envy. "That's some coat you got there, mister. You shoot the buffalo yer- self?"

Noah nodded, wishing the man would go pester someone else and leave him alone. He wasn't in any mood for small talk this afternoon.

"You a rancher hereabouts?"

Noah nodded again, a curt nod.

"Only just moved out here me'self," the man went on. "Don't know many folks yet, takes time. Name's Morris, Henry Morris." He held out a mittened paw.

"Noah Ferguson." Noah shook the extended hand. Any other day, he'd have welcomed this stranger to the Canadian West, taken time to get to know him, but today he was too distracted.

"Nice meetin' ya, Ferguson. Waitin' on my wife Sadie and the kids, comin' out from the East," Morris confided, then waited expectantly.

When Noah didn't respond, Morris shifted from one foot to the other and then gave up. "Well, no sign of the train, and it looks like we're in fer a real blow, way that wind's pickin' up. Don't know about you, but I'm about freezin'. Why not come along inside the station house with the rest of us? No tellin' how late she'll be."

"Thanks. I'll be along presently." Relieved to be left alone, Noah thumped his mittens together and stamped his booted feet, pulling his scarf up and his weathered Western hat further down, painfully aware of the cold on his newly shaven cheeks and chin.

What the hell had possessed him to shave off his beard this morning? His rugged features might look better without all that wild black hair, but the beard might also have kept his chin from freezing, waiting for this damnable train.

And after all, what did he care how he might appear to her? It wasn't as if he had to court her; the marriage was over, the legal bond established between them. She had insisted on a proxy marriage before she left Toronto on the four-day train journey that was bringing her here to Medicine Hat. Against his better judgment—and the advice of the only lawyer in town—Noah had agreed.

He'd wanted it all over and done with. He'd signed the papers and sent the money for the fare, and now that she was almost here, his gut was churning. He wished to God the train would get here so they could be done with this awful first meeting, he and Annie Tompkins.

Annie Ferguson, he corrected himself. Annie Ferguson, his second wife. Tall, she'd described herself. Thirty-four, on the thin side, and plain, which suited him just fine. He'd been relieved to read her description of herself; after all, this was no love match, far from it.

Instead, it was a practical solution for them both. She was a soldier's wife, widowed in the Rebellion of 1885, a farm woman trapped in the city, working in some dingy factory to support herself and her young daughter while longing for the country life she'd known as a child.

And as for him, this marriage was a desperate measure.

He thought of his cranky, bed-ridden father, being cared for at this moment by a kindly neighbor, then deliberately forced his thoughts back to his new wife.

Redheaded, she'd said, which worried Noah some. Was it true, what they said about a redhead's temper? There'd been no sign of it in the eight letters she'd sent during the past months, and Lord only knew he had no experience of women's temper and no desire to learn.

Molly had been the sweetest of women. In their three years of marriage, Noah was hard put to recall times when she'd even come close to losing her temper.

Molly. Without warning, bitter rage at his loss welled up in him, rage so intense that his tall, well-muscled body trembled with the force of it, and he clenched his teeth and knotted his hands into fists inside the blue wool mittens his dead wife had knitted for him.

There were holes worn through one thumb and two fingers. Noah had clumsily mended them.

It had been two years now since Molly and his eighteen-month-old son, Jeremy, had died within hours of one another, victims of typhoid, and in recent months he'd begun to believe this smothering, impotent, choking fury was gone forever, that time had eased the agony of his loss. Instead, here it was back again, as powerful as ever, and now there was this gnawing guilt as well.

I never wanted any woman but you, Molly. Still don't, but I can't do it alone anymore, not since Dad had the stroke. If you'd lived, Molly, I wouldn't be in this damnable position, waiting to meet some stranger. I've had to invite her to share the house we built together, the bed we slept in. Damn it all, Molly, how could you do this to me?

He struggled for, and as always, recovered his self-control. He reminded himself with harsh honesty that his new wife would share as well the work of the ranch, the care of his father, the constant, ill-tempered demands of a once sweet natured man who'd become a tyrant since his stroke.

Noah swallowed hard and the last of the rage subsided, replaced with apprehension. He'd mentioned in his letters to Annie that his father wasn't well, but he'd never really explained exactly what taking care of Zachary involved. Hell, if he had done so, no woman in her right mind would have agreed to come, would she?

Like him, Annie and her young daughter would just have to make the best of this situation. He brushed one hand across his eyes, clearing away the snowflakes that blinded him, and squinted down the track.

Far off down the rails a single headlamp flickered in the driving snowstorm, and over the sound of the wind he could hear the eerie wail of the steam whistle and the sound of an approaching engine. The train was coming.

At last, the waiting was done.

* * *

With a screech of brakes and a cloud of steam, the engine groaned to a halt. Outside the passenger car, it was snowing heavily, but through the frosted window Annie could see a small knot of people on the platform, all-staring expectantly up at the train.

An old man with a white beard was shoveling frantically to clear a path from the platform to the small wooden station.

"Med—i—c—ine Ha-a-a-t," the conductor called in his singsong fashion, making his way down the crowded aisle to open the door.

After four endless days riding across empty wilderness, at last they'd arrived. Heart thumping so hard she was certain it would fly out of her chest, Annie tried to adjust the flamboyant hat Elinora had given her as a parting gift, but it wouldn't stay put.

Bets reached out and straightened it, and Annie gave her a grateful smile and a wink, trying to pretend a bravado she was far from feeling. With trembling hands she gathered their bundles together, wrapped Bets's wool shawl tighter around her, and followed the other departing passengers to the door.

Tilting her chin high, Annie lifted her skirts and stepped down into snow on legs that had turned to jelly.

Lordie, it was freezing. She paused and caught her breath as the cold air seared her lungs. Once the first shock was over, however, the icy air felt clean and invigorating after the stuffy train compartment, but it started Bets to coughing again.

Annie twisted her sister's scarf up and over her chin and mouth, and then, feeling sick with nerves, she squinted into the snow and tried to pick out which of the men waiting a short distance away might be Noah Ferguson.

Thirty-six years old, he'd written. Tall, dark-haired.

Her eyes skittered past a short, round figure with a cable knit hat pulled down to his eyelids, lingered on a thin, red-faced man with a handlebar moustache and a brimmed cap, and then settled on the giant standing like a statue a little distance from the others, brimmed hat hiding his face, hands thrust deep into the pockets of a huge furry coat. Annie looked, and looked again.

Some sixth sense told her that this was her husband.

His gaze touched her face and flicked past her, to the passenger car where a very fat woman with several children was now being helped down the step. "Sadie," bellowed the man in the knitted hat, racing over and throwing his arms around her.

There were no other passengers getting off. The conductor was closing the door.

The man in the heavy coat looked at Annie again, puzzlement in his frown, and Annie swallowed hard and said a silent, fervent prayer as he moved towards her.

Lordie, he was big. She was tall for a woman, but he towered over her. There was a ruggedness and raw strength about him unfamiliar to Annie, accustomed as she was to city men.

She drew herself up and squared her shoulders, praying that she didn't look as terrified as she felt. She attempted a smile and knew it was a dismal failure.

"How do you do?" Her voice was barely audible.

His face was all angles and planes, a stern, strong, handsome face, clean shaven and unsmiling.

"I'm looking for Miss Annie Tompkins. Rather, Mrs. Annie Ferguson," he corrected. His voice was a deep baritone.

"That's me," she managed to say. She tried again to smile, but her lips felt paralyzed. "I'm Annie, and this is my—this is Bets."

Bets, her wide, feverish blue gaze intent on Noah's face, made a small curtsy and then edged fearfully behind her sister, doing her best to stifle her coughing and not succeeding.

Annie cleared her throat; desperately trying to remember the dignified little speech she'd been preparing every anxious moment since she'd left Toronto. Not one word came to her.

"Hello, Noah Ferguson," she finally managed to stammer.

"Pleased to meet you, I'm sure," she choked out, painfully aware that she sounded both weak-minded and simpering.

He didn't respond. Instead, his coal-dark eyes slowly took in her hat, her face, then her figure. He looked her up and down. Annie refused to flinch under his gaze. She clenched her teeth as he stepped around her to stare at Bets before he once again turned his attention to Annie.

"You're considerably younger than you led me to believe, madam. How old are you, exactly?" He was scowling down at her, and a shiver ran down her spine that had nothing to do with the snow swirling around them.

Here it was then, the first consequence of all her lying. There was nothing to be done except confront it head on.

"I'm twenty-two." Annie tilted her chin as high as she could and met his coal-dark eyes, but after a long moment under his steady gaze, her bravado crumbled.

"Well, almost twenty-two. I'll be twenty-one this June." At the thunderous look on his face, she hurriedly added, "I know you wanted someone older, Mr. Ferguson. I was afraid if I told the truth, you wouldn't have me. Us. But I assure you, I feel a lot older inside than my years. If that's any help."

He actually snorted in disgust. He looked from her to Bets and back again. "Twenty years old. And with a fourteen-year-old daughter? That's quite an accomplishment, madam." His voice dripped with sarcasm.

If it weren't so cold, Annie would have sworn this was hell.

"She's—Bets is my little sister, not my daughter," she confessed miserably. "I—I've never been married. I thought you might not—I thought—"

He stared at her until she gulped and was silent. "You thought I was fair game, and you told me only what you figured I wanted to hear. I take it most of what you've told me about yourself is nothing but a pack of lies. Is that so, madam?"

His voice was quiet, but lethal.

Annie desperately wanted to contradict him, but couldn't. The fact was, a great deal of what she'd told him was a pack of lies. There was no denying it.

"Some," she admitted miserably. "The part about growing up on a farm wasn't exactly honest. But the part about me and Bets being hard workers, that's the god-honest truth," she burst out. "We worked from dawn to dusk in Lazenby's cotton mill, anybody could tell you we were among the best. Just give us a chance, and we'll prove it to you, Mr. Ferguson, I promise we will."

"If I'd wanted farmhands, I'd have hired men." He looked as though he was about to explode, and Annie steeled herself.

Bets had been choking back her coughing, but now it took hold of her with a vengeance and she doubled over, her face purple.

Annie drew the smaller girl close against her side and felt Bets's whole body trembling. The wind had picked up and the snow was swirling around them.

Annie had been too distraught to even feel the cold, but now it suddenly thrust icy fingers past the inadequate barrier of her clothing, and she was miserably aware that the soles on her boots were worn through in places, letting the snow in.

"My sister's sick, Mr. Ferguson. She caught the grippe on the train, and we're both freezing cold. Please, couldn't we talk this over at some later time?"

Annie knew the moment had come when he could— probably would—turn his back on them and simply walk away. She knew he'd be well within his rights to do that very thing, leaving them to fend for themselves in a snowstorm in the middle of the wild Canadian west.

Desperation gripped her. If he left them, what in God's name would she do? She had little money left; she knew no one in this barren, savage place. All she'd ever done was work in the cotton mill, and she was pretty certain there were no mills within a thousand miles of here.

She was terrified. She trembled with fear, and her stomach churned. She clutched Bets's arm so tightly that the girl cried out.

Ferguson's eyes held hers for what seemed an eternity, and with her last vestige of courage, Annie stared straight back, willing him—begging him, entreating him—to give her a chance.

Chapter Two

Warm in his heavy coat, utterly furious at being deceived, Noah was suddenly conscious that the woman and her sister were shivering. He noted that their coats were thin, and they were poorly dressed for temperatures below freezing. The ridiculous hat with the bird's nest on it seemed about to blow away in the wind.

Annie was holding on to it with one arm and hugging her sister with the other.

The girl coughed again, hollow and harsh, and the ferocity of it coming from such a skinny little kid shocked him and added to the impotent anger he felt at his proxy bride.

The lying little trollop had saddled him with still another invalid, if the sound of that cough was any indication. The girl sounded as if she might have consumption.

The irony of the situation brought a grim smile. At least he needn't feel guilt any longer about Zachary. Annie Tompkins had far outdone him in duplicity.

Her lies were grounds for annulling the marriage, he knew that. He need have no qualms about washing his hands of both her and her ailing sister right there and then. No court in the land would say different.

But where would he be then? Noah raged. It would take months to get a response to a new advertisement, and spring wasn't that far off, with its dawn- to-dusk clearing and ploughing and planting of hay. There was his prized herd of cattle to tend to, chores to finish with no time or energy left at the end of the day to prepare meals and do the endless tasks a household seemed to require . . . tasks he had no skill for and despised. And most important of all, worst of all, there was his father, bedridden, needing constant attention and care.

He'd already hired two people in the past six months, one an elderly spinster he'd brought out from Lethbridge and the other a young Englishman, a drifter. Both had quit after only one week of dealing with his father.

It had become all too obvious to Noah that he urgently needed a wife. Wives didn't just quit when things were tough.

But women of any sort were a rare commodity out here on the Canadian prairies, which was why he'd finally advertised in the blasted Toronto newspaper in the first place. And there hadn't been much choice, when it came down to it; the only other woman besides Annie who answered his ad had been the widowed mother of six small children.

It seemed he was well and truly stuck with her. Lies or not, he urgently needed this woman he'd married. At the very least, he'd have to postpone judgment for a few days, perhaps a week.

With great reluctance, he decided he'd take her and her sister out to the ranch, and if the situation proved truly intolerable, he'd buy them a train ticket back to the city.

His voice was harsh. "Get inside the depot and get yourselves warm while I bring the horse and wagon around. The station master'll give you hot coffee. Is that your luggage over there?" He pointed down the platform, where a single tin trunk and several carpetbags were all that was left of the pile unloaded from the baggage car.

At Annie's timid nod, he turned on his heel and made his way past the depot and down the street to the livery stable, cursing himself for being a softhearted fool.

Afterwards, Annie had only fragmented memories of the long, snowy ride to the homestead.

He'd been thoughtful enough—in the back of the wagon, he'd made a cozy nest for them from heavy buffalo robes he'd brought along, placing their trunk so it blocked some of the wind. He'd lifted Bets as if she were as light as a snowflake and plunked her into the wagon.

Annie grabbed her long skirts and started clambering in by herself, but suddenly his hands grasped her waist, and she too was lifted, none too gently, up and over the backboard. He said not a single word. She stowed her hat safely beside her and snuggled down beside her sister amidst the smoky, wild smelling fur robes. The wagon tilted as he climbed up on the seat and clucked to the horse.

Annie peeked out as they lumbered through the small frontier town, past a building that said Post Office, then a two-story log building with a sign proclaiming "Lansdowne Hotel." The rest of the town was made up of a few frame houses, numerous shacks, and even a dozen tents. They crossed a narrow steel bridge that spanned a river almost covered in ice and finally set off across an expanse of frozen prairie.

For a while, Annie worried about Indians. She knew that the red-coated Mounted Policemen had brought law and order to this barren land several years ago, but she didn't see any around here.

She didn't see any Indians either, so after a while she worried instead about how Noah Ferguson knew which direction to take. The whole flat, bleak landscape looked exactly the same to her in every direction, cold and gray and empty, dreary beyond measure. She'd never imagined this much space with so little in it. She realized after a time that he was more or less following the path of the frozen river.

Slowly, despite the cold wind and the snow whirling around them, Annie's body grew warm beneath the heavy covering. The fatigue of the long train journey coupled with intense relief at not being deserted at the depot combined to make her sleepy.

Bets had already cuddled close beside her beneath the heavy robe. She was sound asleep, and at last Annie too put her head under the covering, pulling it over the two of them until only a small space remained for fresh air.

It was dark inside. It smelled strange, but it was like being safe in a warm cave with a storm raging outside. She slept, an uneasy sleep interrupted by the sound of the wind, the jingle of the harness, and the occasional word of encouragement spoken by Ferguson to his horse.

His voice and the fierce, joyful barking of a dog startled her awake. "Hello there, old Jake," she heard him say. "Good dog, good boy."

She stuck her head out, shocked to discover how dark it had become. The snow seemed to have
stopped, but the air was frigid.

The wagon was still moving, but past Noah's shoulder Annie could see a substantial log house directly ahead with light in the windows, and the dark outlines of numerous other buildings scattered nearby. The dog, large and black, was barking madly and running alongside the wagon.

"Quiet, Jake, good dog." At Noah's order, the dog stopped barking, running close beside them with his tail wagging hard.

Bets, too, was awake now. Eyes still heavy with fever, she peered around and then took Annie's mittened hand in her own and squeezed it. Annie gave her a reassuring smile.

The wagon stopped. Noah jumped down and came around, lifting first Annie and then Bets to the snowy ground.

"Go ahead in," he instructed. "Tell Gladys Hopkins I'll take her home right away."

Stiff from the hours in the wagon, Annie staggered up the steps and across the porch to the door, Bets's hand tight in her own. It was thrown open before she could decide whether to knock. Inside was a small, round woman with a neat brown bun on the top of her head, prominent blue eyes, and a wide, welcoming smile. She looked perhaps a dozen years older than Annie. The room behind her was warm and smelled of food cooking.

"Well, so here you are. Welcome to you." Already wrapping herself in a black coat and holding a red checkered shawl, the woman closed the door behind them with a bang. "No sense heatin' the world, I always say. I'm Gladys Hopkins, we're Noah's neighbors west of here. So you're the new Mrs. Ferguson. Noah already said your name was Annie." Her bright eyes were kind and curious. "And who might you be, dearie?" She smiled at Bets.

"This is Betsy Tompkins, my sister," Annie supplied hurriedly. "Pleased to meet you, Mrs. Hopkins."

"You call me Gladys, I'll call you Annie. We're gonna be friends. Goodness knows we're the only white women this side of the Hat. Sorry I have to hurry off like this, but it's fixin' to storm, and I got a husband and a daughter waitin' on their supper. I left soup and fresh bread on the warmer over there fer you."

She gestured to the cookstove against the wall and then tied the red wool scarf over her hair. She leaned close to

Annie, whispering in her ear, "The old man in there's had his supper. Didn't eat enough to keep a sparrow alive. He's in a right fair temper, same as always these days. Don't you let him get the best of you now, dearie."

At that moment, the door opened and Noah came in with the tin trunk.

Gladys jumped back and said in a loud, guilty voice, "I'll come visitin' soon as the weather allows. Hope you settle in fine, Annie. My stars, would you look at this snow? Bye-bye, now, Betsy." She went out quickly, closing the door behind her.

Noah thumped the trunk on the floor, returning a moment later with the carpetbags and her hat, which he dumped unceremoniously on top of the trunk.

"Make yourselves right at home," he said, and Annie flushed, recognizing sarcasm when she heard it. "It'll take me at least three hours to get back, and then, madam, I'd say you have some explaining to do."

Before Annie could begin to think of a response, the door slammed shut behind him and she and Bets were alone. She closed her eyes for a moment and breathed a sigh of relief. At least she'd have time to gather her wits about her before she had to face him again. He was downright formidable.

For a few moments, they busied themselves with taking off their coats and shawls and boots. They hung their things on the pegs by the door, then stood side by side, looking wide-eyed around the large, pleasant room, each silently comparing it with the small, cramped space they'd shared in the city.

Noah Ferguson had written that he wasn't well off, but to Annie, this looked like a grand house indeed.

The area was softly lit by a coal-oil lamp that had roses on the glass shade. The lamp was set on a crocheted doily on a high dresser beneath a window.

The room, a very large combination kitchen and living room, had a huge iron cook stove presiding at one end and a wood heater at the other. Both were giving off waves of comforting warmth, and Annie and Bets moved hesitantly to stand by the heater and warm themselves.

There was a square wooden table and four chairs near the cook stove, and a horsehair sofa and a rocking chair at the opposite end of the room where a narrow staircase led to another floor. There were several cross-stitched pillows on the sofa, and a border of hand-embroidered roses trimmed the white fabric of the curtains at the window. The wooden floor had several braided rag rugs, and there was floral wallpaper on the walls. An ornate clock sat on a shelf specially made for it. Also on the walls were several pictures clipped from magazines and carefully mounted on cardboard.

Everywhere Annie looked was the mark of a woman who'd made this house into a cozy home.

Noah Ferguson had told Annie in his first letter that he was a widower, that his wife and baby son had died two years before.

It was obvious that Noah's wife had loved this house, Annie thought uneasily. Her touch was everywhere, although as Annie looked more closely, there was also a general air of neglect. There was a thick layer of dust on the dresser, and the curtains were limp with dirt. Although the wide boards on the floor showed signs of a recent sweeping, it was plain they hadn't been scrubbed in some time.

Near the heater were two doors. One was shut, but the other was ajar, and suddenly, a loud banging came from behind it, as though someone was hammering on the floor with a heavy object.

"Lordie, that scared me." Annie's hand went to her heart. "I forgot there was anybody else here."

Bets's eyes were wide and fearful.

"I think it's Mr. Ferguson's father," Annie indicated. "I will see to him. You warm yourself by the fire."

Hesitantly, she tapped at the door and then pushed it open so she could enter the small room. It was painted blue, and on the wall was a picture of a smiling cherub cuddling a kitten. A chair, a dresser, and the single bed took up most of the space.

"Mr. Ferguson?" Annie said in a hesitant tone, standing beside the bed. "I'm—I'm Annie. I've only just arrived. Is there something you want?"

The white-haired man lying propped on pillows in the disheveled bed held a cane tight in his right fist. When he saw Annie, he lifted it up and brandished it threateningly, making strange guttural noises in his throat.

She cried out and leaped back, certain he was about to strike her.

His face was twisted grotesquely to one side, and it was plain to Annie that his right hand and side were useless. It was also obvious that he was in a furious temper.

Annie stared at him, horrified. Was he a madman? Noah Ferguson had mentioned his father in his letters, but all he'd said was that the older man was "in ill health."

He stopped trying to speak and lay back panting, staring at Annie with the same coal-black, angry look his son had given her earlier.

"Can—can I get you something, sir?" she asked again.

He used the end of the cane to gesture at a water glass and Annie cautiously sidled over and snatched it up.

"Water? I'll bring it directly." She backed out of the room, expecting at any moment that he'd throw the cane at her.

In the outer room, Bets was coughing again, huddled in an exhausted heap on a chair by the fire. Annie went over and felt her head.

"You're burning up. We need to get you to bed, sweets."

She filled the water glass from the pail on the washstand, but before she could take it back into the bedroom, the awful hammering began again.

Annie rolled her eyes and blew her breath out in an exasperated *whoosh.* He was trying her patience, that was certain.

She walked quickly back into the bedroom and over to the bed, holding out the glass. In a firm tone, she said, "Here you go, and I'd be grateful if you'd please stop that banging, Mr. Ferguson."

The old man made a grumbling noise, put the cane on the bed beside him and snatched at the glass with his good hand, but he misjudged and bumped Annie's arm. The glass spilled, sloshing most of the water on the patchwork quilt that covered him.

With a roar of absolute rage, he grabbed the glass and flung it against the blue-painted wall. It smashed into shards, and Annie let out a shriek and ran for the door. Trembling, she closed it firmly behind her, and the now-familiar thumping began again.

She wasn't going back, she told herself. Thirsty or not, he'd have to wait until his son came home and tended to him.

With the constant banging as accompaniment, Annie set out bowls, and she and Bets ate the thick, aromatic soup simmering on the back of the cook stove. A loaf of freshly baked bread stayed warm beneath a snowy napkin, and there was butter in a bowl.

Annie sent Gladys a heartfelt thank-you, but the incessant banging was difficult to ignore, and her hand trembled as she spooned up the soup and spread butter on a slice of the crusty bread.

Bets ate only a spoonful of soup, took several bites of bread, then sank back in her chair, exhausted.

The young girl needed rest, but where would she put Bets to sleep? Hurriedly finishing her meal, Annie lit a candle and peeked into the other ground-floor bedroom. It was obviously Noah's room; his clothing hung on wall pegs, and two pair of immense boots stood side by side on the floor.

Feeling like an intruder, Annie stepped inside, swallowing hard as she looked at the wide double bed. Her mind's eye filled now with the image of the muscular giant who, in name at least, was her husband. Her cheeks grew hot at the thought of climbing into that bed beside him.

"I'd say you have some explaining to do, madam." His parting words echoed in her head. *Well, Mr. Ferguson, you have a bit of explaining to do yourself,* she concluded. *Such as why you didn't tell me the facts about that impossible old man.*

Next she ventured up the staircase with her candle, anticipating an unfinished loft, drafty and primitive. There were two doors, and when she opened the one on the right, her eyes widened and she caught her breath with pleasure.

Here was a cozy little gabled room with a single bed covered with a warm quilt. There was a beautiful old dresser against the wall and a rocking chair beside the window. A wooden chest stood at the foot of the bed, hand-carved in a beautiful pattern of birds and flowers. It was the gnarled pipe and the tin of tobacco resting on top of the chest that told Annie this must have been the old man's room before he became ill.

She looked around again, more carefully this time. In a corner was a box of wood-carving tools and several small blocks of wood, one of them half carved into the rough shape of a bird. She remembered the twisted claw that was his hand, and she felt a stab of compassion for the wild old man trapped in the bedroom downstairs.

She peeked behind the other door before she went down.

It was an unfinished attic, and the candle sent eerie flickers of light over a cradle, a high chair, a box spilling over with toys—sad reminders that a baby had lived in this house not long ago.

Annie loved babies. Her throat grew tight and she quickly shut the door and hurried downstairs.

In front of the heater, she helped Bets take off her clothing. Her sister was exhausted and sick. Annie sponged her down quickly from a basin, rubbing her dry with a clean hessian towel she found in the drawer of the washstand. From their trunk, she took a thick flannel nightdress and fresh under drawers and bundled her sister into them. She urged Bets up the stairs and then tucked her into bed in the cozy little room, pressing a kiss on her sister's flushed cheek. Bets sighed and was asleep in seconds.

Downstairs, Annie realized that at some point the floor banging had stopped. She tiptoed to the old man's door and peeked in. He was snoring heavily, cane propped beside the bed, damp quilt thrown on the floor. She drew the covers up over him, blew out the lamp, and brought the damp quilt to dry by the heater.

The farmhouse was silent except for the crackling of the flames in the two stoves and the occasional gust of wind outside.

More than anything, Annie wanted a wash, and she'd better hurry, before *he* got back.

She stripped off every scrap of her soiled clothing and lathered a cloth from the bar of yellow soap. Luxuriously, beginning with her face and working downward, she methodically washed and rinsed every inch of herself, glorying in the wonderful sensation of being clean again.

Her bone-thin body ached as if every muscle had been strained to the breaking point, and she longed to be able to lie down somewhere and sleep as Bets was doing, but she didn't dare give in to the bone-crushing weariness. She couldn't even put on a nightdress. She opened her trunk and found a clean dress, underwear, and stockings, and put them on.

She intended to stay alert, because when Noah Ferguson returned, he wasn't going to get the best of her.

She glanced at the room where the old man slept, and shuddered.

Maybe she'd been less than honest in her letters, but it seemed that Noah Ferguson wasn't far behind her when it came to leaving out important details.

Annie's mouth tilted in a rueful grin.

Maybe after all was said and done, the pair of them were made for each other after all.

Chapter Three

The wind had quieted, but it was black-dark and icy cold by the time Noah again drove into his farmyard late that evening.

He was in a foul mood. Gladys Hopkins, kind as she was, talked far too much. All the way to the Hopkins homestead, she'd blathered on and on, all of it about his new wife.

"That red hair of hers is a caution, don't you think, Noah? And she looks mighty frail, poor soul. Makes a body wonder if folks in the city get enough to eat, don't it?"

Noah made an indeterminate noise in his throat and clicked his tongue, flicking the reins so the team would go faster.

Unfortunately, Gladys went right on talking.

"But those eyes, my stars, Noah, I never in all my born days saw eyes that shade of green before. Must be what the books call emerald, wouldn't you say? And big like saucers, why they seem to swallow her whole face, don't they? Long eyelashes too. Awful pale complexion, though. Needs some good old farm grub to fatten her up some. Now how old did you say she was, again?"

Fortunately, he hadn't said, and he didn't now. "Old enough to wed," he growled. *Old enough to deceive an honest man.*

Gladys wasn't in the least put out. "Her sister's a quiet little thing, ain't she? Not a single word out of her. Looks to be about the same age as my Rose. Rosie's gonna be over the moon when she hears there's a girl her age over at your place. She'll pester me to death wantin' to visit. Now, Noah, my experience with girls that age is they never stop talking. Just you wait till she gets over her fit of shyness, won't be a quiet moment. I think you did good, the two of them will be a big help with Zachary, that's certain." She paused for a moment, then added in a different tone, "Your poor old dad ain't doin' too good, is he? You sure had your share of trouble, Noah, first Molly and the boy, and now Zachary."

Damnation. With all the goings on, Noah hadn't given a single thought to the inevitable meeting between the two females and his father. He felt a twinge of apprehension and a renewed surge of guilt. He ought to at least have warned Annie.

"How was he today, Gladys?" Noah fervently hoped that Zachary was having one of his rare quiet periods, but Gladys's response settled that idea.

"Contrary. Threw a cup at me, he did," she said with a sigh. "And he banged that infernal cane on the floor most of the day. It beats all how a kind, sweet gentleman like your father was could turn so willful now he's sick," she commented with a shake of her head.

"Mind you, I recollect Harold's aunt, sweetest old thing—"

Noah was relieved beyond measure when at last Gladys was safely inside her own house and he was free to ride home in silence. Trouble was, some of what she'd prattled on about seemed stuck in his head.

Annie did have amazing green eyes, he conceded. And some secret part of him was immensely relieved that she wasn't grossly fat.   He preferred a slender woman. He wondered what all that wild, curling hair would be like, loose down her back.

The need for a woman in his bed had been growing more urgent as time blurred the pain of Molly's death. Part of him had been anticipating the bodily pleasure of having a woman beneath him again.

But this woman—well, it wasn't at all certain she'd be staying, he reminded himself. God only knew what the real facts were about her, and until he knew for certain, he'd not be beguiled by the demands of a healthy body.

A horrible thought struck him. Maybe she'd lied about working in the mill. Maybe she'd been a strumpet, a woman of easy virtue.

But reason asserted itself. Surely there was something about her, a kind of innocence, that would be impossible to pretend?

But what was the truth? He was convinced that hardly one single thing she'd said about herself in those damnable letters was the least bit honest. At the thought of her duplicity, he grew angry all over again, and he held firmly to his righteous outrage the rest of the drive home.

Once there, he tended to the horses in the bam, threw hay down for the livestock and, finally, headed for the house. For the first time, he didn't feel his usual pleasure and anticipation about coming home. He was troubled more than he cared to admit about the forthcoming scene with the woman inside.

As he climbed the porch steps and opened the door, he remembered something a friend had said about a neighbor's marital trouble: "Marry in haste, repent at leisure."

Noah's mouth twisted in a bitter smile as he opened the door. It seemed there was a lot of truth to the old saw after all.

He wasn't sure exactly what he expected, but to his immense relief, all was quiet, peaceful, and blessedly warm inside. The room was tidy, and the table was set for his meal.

There was silence from his father's room and no sign of the younger girl. Annie was curled in a ball on the sofa, sound asleep.

The door banged when he closed it. She let out a small cry of alarm and sat bolt upright, sleepy green eyes wide and startled.

She was wearing a clean but rumpled blue checked dress, and her hair was even wilder than before, curling in fiery disarray around her face and neck. She reached up to tidy it, and he couldn't help but notice the slight, delicate curves of her body.

She wasn't wearing shoes or slippers; all she had on her narrow, long feet were white cotton stockings that seemed more mends than fabric. There was a fragility about her that threatened to soften the hardness in his heart if he weren't careful.

"Hello." He bent to remove his boots. He hung his coat and hat up and made his way to the washstand, rolling up shirt and underwear sleeves and lathering his face, neck, and arms thoroughly. He tugged a comb through his thick, tangled hair without so much as a glance in the wavy mirror on the wall above the basin.

He didn't give a damn what she thought about the way he looked, he told himself sternly.

"I put Bets to bed in the room at the top of the stairs. I hope that's all right," she said.

He nodded. "It was my father's room. I had to move him down when the first housekeeper came. Her legs were bad and she couldn't climb up and down the steps." He didn't add that the little room his father now occupied had once belonged to his baby son. He'd packed the cradle and the tiny clothing, along with Molly's things, up to the attic and never set foot there again.

"You have a lovely house," she said shyly, and added, "Your dinner's waiting."

She'd set a place for him at the table, and now she filled a bowl with hot soup and put sliced bread in front of him. "You want coffee?"

"Yes, please." He'd grown accustomed to serving himself. It was pleasant to have her see to his needs.

She filled a cup from the enamel pot on the back of the stove and set it before him along with a pitcher of milk. When his needs were tended to, she poured herself coffee as well and took the chair opposite him at the table.

"The storm's stopped," she said in a conversational tone.

"Yes, it's died down. Temperature's dropping, though. It'll be a cold night."

Obviously, she'd decided to postpone serious discussion until after he'd eaten, and he was grateful. He was as hungry as a wolf. He spooned in the delicious soup, sopping up the juice with thick slabs of bread. She sipped her coffee and refilled his soup bowl before he could ask, and once she got up and restocked the heater. In spite of himself, he noticed how quick she was, lithe and light on her feet.

When at last he was comfortably full, he sat back with a second mug of coffee, wondering just where to begin, and while he pondered, she bested him.

"I made your father's acquaintance," she said in a quiet tone. "He wanted water, and when I brought it, he spilled it and threw the glass at me. I didn't clean up the splinters. I was afraid he might take it in his head to hit me with that cane if I ventured back in there. He's not very easy to get on with."

So instead of accusing her the way he'd planned, Noah somehow found himself on the defensive. "My father had a stroke just before Christmas. Before that, he was a strong and independent man."

He'd also been Noah's best friend. "He finds it hard to be bedridden and helpless."

She gave him a level look. "I can understand that. It's a terrible thing to depend on other people for everything. But you didn't tell me how sick he really was, in your letters. You said he was in ill health, but I took that to mean he'd get better. Is he going to?"

He blew out his breath and shook his head, holding her gaze. It was hard to put into words, hard to believe even after all these months, that his father had become the pitiful, angry man in the bed in the other room. The agony in Noah's heart made it hard to speak. "No. This is pretty much how it's going to be, according to Doc Witherspoon."

She nodded slowly, a frown creasing her brow. "And he needs a whole lot of caring for." It wasn't a question.

A muscle in Noah's jaw twitched as he saw the direction this was taking. "Yes, he does." His voice was dangerously quiet. She wasn't about to have this her own way. He took control again, his voice harsh. "And I don't suppose you know any more about taking care of sick folks than you do about farming," he said.

"Matter of fact, I do." She lifted her chin and looked him square in the eye. "My mama was sick for two years before she died, and between us Bets and I cared for her as well as we knew. The last few months, she couldn't get out of bed either."

"And where was your father?" He watched her closely, wondering how he'd even know if she was lying again.

She met his eyes, honest and forthright, and her full lips tightened. Her expression made her look much older suddenly. "He was drunk, mostly. He wasn't mean, like some who drink, just sad and useless. He never could keep a job very long."

Noah knew of men who drank. He enjoyed a whisky now and then, but along with all the other things Zach had taught him was a respect for spirits and what they could do to a man.

"How did you live?"

"My mama was a seamstress, a good one. She managed to feed us and pay the rent until she got sick," Annie said. "Then I got the job in the factory, and that helped. But after Mama died, I couldn't manage any more to feed us and pay the rent, so Bets had to start working too." A haunted look came and went on her face. "Bets isn't as strong as me. The air's bad in a factory, and she coughed a lot."

She interpreted the look on his face and added defensively, "She isn't an invalid, honest. All she needs is some fresh air and good food, and she'll be fine again. She hasn't got consumption, or anything bad like that."

He didn't comment, because he had his doubts. Instead, he went doggedly on. "You said in one letter that your father was dead. Is that true?" What if her sop of a n'er-do-well father turned up, looking to Noah to support him? He shuddered. There were aspects to this proxy marriage that Noah had never thought about till now.

But she answered promptly, and unless she was an accomplished actress, Noah was convinced she was being honest.

"Papa's been dead four years now. He fell and hit his head one night coming from the tavern, and he died the next day."

It was a relief to hear it, although naturally Noah didn't say so.

"Who taught you to read and write?" He'd been impressed by her letter-writing ability, and he found himself liking the proper way she talked. She sounded educated, a rare thing in a woman of her background.

"My mama taught both my sister and me," she said proudly. "Her father was a schoolteacher. He taught her. We had books."

"Reading's fine, but do you know how to cook?" He was plain fed up with the meals he was forced to throw together. They'd given him a new respect for good food.

She hesitated. "Some. A little. Plain food, mostly. We never had money for anything fancy. Bets is real good at making soup."

"You said you grew up on a farm," he went on relentlessly. "You talked of making butter, of milking cows, of growing a garden." More lies, he reminded himself again. "How'd you know what to say about those things?"

She looked down at the table, her finger circling a mark on the cloth. "I have a good friend, our landlady, Elinora Potts. Elinora grew up on a farm. She helped me." She raised her eyes and met his accusing gaze with rebellious courage. "See, I'd answered three other advertisements before yours, and I was truthful in them, and not one man wrote back to me."

So he'd been the bottom of the barrel. It wasn't exactly flattering, but somehow it amused him.

"Don't you see, Mr. Ferguson, I just had to get Bets out of there?" she went on, her voice trembling. "She'd have *died*." She leaned her arms on the table and bent towards him, intent on making him understand. "Have you ever been inside a cotton factory, Mr. Ferguson?"

He shook his head no. He was intrigued by the fierce passion in her voice, the fire smoldering in her green eyes. Against his will, he was drawn to her. Whatever else she was, she was wholly alive and very female, this Annie.

She didn't seem to notice that he shifted uncomfortably in his chair.

"Cotton factories aren't healthy. The air's full of lint, it's hot all the time; a shift's twelve hours with only a few minutes for lunch, and you've got to pay close attention every second. Many girls are injured or killed at the machines. Wintertime, you never see daylight at all." She tapped a forefinger against her chest. "Me, I'm tough."

The assertion made Noah want to smile. She sat there, in her washed-out blue dress, her body so thin it seemed a good wind would blow her away.

"I got used to it. But Bets—" her eyes welled with sudden tears and she brushed them away with her palm. "She's my baby sister, Mr. Ferguson. I promised Mama I'd take care of her." There was a desperate plea in her voice, and Noah couldn't help the flood of sympathy her words aroused.

"When I saw your advertisement, it felt like a last chance to save her. I—I was scared. She was coughing all the time. She's all I have for family. So I"— the rest of the sentence burst out in a flurry of words—"well, that's why I wasn't honest in most of what I told you."

In spite of himself, her story touched him, but he didn't let any of what he felt show on his face. A great deal depended on the next few moments, and he didn't want to make a mistake that would be hard to rectify.

He narrowed his eyes at her, and his voice was deliberately harsh. "The last thing I need is another invalid in this house. Life out here in the West is tough. It takes able-bodied people all their time just to survive. Far as I can see, you didn't give much thought to that when you brought your sister here. There's drought and frost and pestilence, hail storms that can level a man's crops. There's wild animals and

Indians that can kill him and his family. There's no one to call on for help. It's a half-day's drive into town and an hour and a half just to get to the Hopkins place. Ranching is backbreaking hard work for everybody. Come spring, I'll be in the fields from sunup to sundown."

"I told you I was a good worker," she pleaded. "I'll prove it if you give me a chance. Just tell me what you need done, and I'll do my best."

"I don't want any misunderstandings about how hard it will be." Noah drew in a breath and let it out again. "You've seen how my father is," he said deliberately. "I'd expect you to take good care of him in spite of his temper. You'd have to tend to all the household chores, the chickens, the garden, the pigs. If I can't get a hired hand, I'll need you to help with haying in the fall. My advice would be to take your sister and hightail it back to the city."

She stared at him, waiting for him to go on. When he didn't she said in a hesitant tone, "You're trying to scare me off, aren't you? You're leaving it for me to decide whether we should stay or go."

Noah nodded. "I am. And now that you know exactly how it would be, seems to me you should give some serious thought to leaving."

She eyed him warily, as if there were a trap here somewhere. "But you're not sending us back?"

He shook his head. "I can't say I'm entirely happy with the way things turned out, but the simple fact is, I need help. I need a wife." It was the raw, honest truth.

She looked into his face, her wide-spaced eyes somber. After a moment she lifted her chin and said firmly, "Then we're staying. I'm used to hard work, like I said. Besides," she added as her eyes dropped to the oilcloth and her voice became suddenly less certain than before, "we—we're married, you and I, before God."

He nodded. "We are that." Something inside him eased, relieved at her words.

"There's one more thing, though." She was agitated, twisting a bit of her skirt between her fingers, unable to look at him now. "There's another thing I didn't tell you that probably will make you—make you change your mind after all. I—I was wrong, not telling you before," she added, and for the first time, there was outright panic in her voice. "You have to know, you'll find out anyway soon enough," she added miserably.

Her expression, the quaver in her voice, told him that this was far more significant than anything else she'd lied about. Noah felt his stomach clench. What terrible thing was she about to reveal?

"It's—it's—ummm, it's my sister, Bets." Now her words tumbled out, one on top of the other. "She's— she's the sweetest girl, and smart as a whip, but— well, she got a fever when she was a baby, not even two years old." She still wasn't meeting his eyes, and he frowned, confused.

He'd expected some damning, shoddy confession about herself, and instead Annie was talking about her sister? Puzzlement furrowed his brow.

"After it left her—the fever, I mean—well, she— she couldn't—she didn't—she was—" her eyes were enormous as they met to his. "Bets didn't hear us anymore." Her breath came out in a quavering sigh. "It affected her ears. What I didn't tell you was that my sister is stone deaf, Mr. Ferguson."

Chapter Four

A log fell in the stove, and from the bedroom came the muffled sound of Zachary snoring.

Noah stared across the table at this woman he'd married, feeling the strangest mixture of compassion, impatience, desire—and outrage.

What miserable kind of man did she take him for, to think that her sister's affliction was something he couldn't accept? The other things she'd lied about, her knowledge of farming life, for instance, those things were serious, they would mean he'd have to take precious time to teach her all the things he'd thought she already knew. But deafness . . .

"Having a deaf sister seems to me to be a fact of life and nothing to feel shame over," he said, and his reward was the astonished relief that slowly mirrored itself on her mobile features.

"There are practical matters to consider, of course," he added. "Does she talk?"

Annie shook her head. "She makes sounds, but they're hard to understand. She lip-reads well, and we have hand signals that mean different things. They're not hard to learn," she assured him eagerly. "I can easily teach you, if you want to learn."

He nodded. "I do. I want there to be good understanding between me and the girl."

Annie suddenly seemed to droop, like a candle burning down. Her shoulders, held high and tense, relaxed now, and her hands fell to her lap. Her full lips parted, and the small, worried crease between her delicate brows smoothed away.

"I do thank you, Mr. Ferguson," she breathed, her voice husky and low. "I truly think you are a kind, good man."

Noah's face reddened at her compliment, and he cleared his throat, embarrassed. "Enough of this calling me Mr. Ferguson," he said gruffly. "It makes me feel old and downright doddery. Call me Noah."

"All right, Noah," she said with a quick, almost mischievous grin.

"Annie," he responded formally, trying the feel of it on his tongue and lips.

Annie, his wedded wife.

They sat in silence for several long, charged minutes, each realizing that what had passed between them just now was a commitment, a true beginning to their life together.

Whatever the future held, they would face it united.

Not with bonds of love, Noah assured himself, never that, never again, but instead, those of responsibility, of mutual commitment to the common purpose of making a decent life for themselves in a difficult land.

The clock chimed eleven and Noah stood up, uncomfortably aware that although they'd crossed one dangerous abyss, another yawned right in front of them.

"Time for bed." He did his best to make it casual, but there was a tension in his tone he couldn't seem to hide. There was also tension in his body, anticipating the act he'd missed so sorely for so long.

She nodded and rose, and he could see the flush that crept from the demure neck of her gown all the way to her hairline. Her eyes slid toward the door of his bedroom and away.

New questions sprang into his mind, questions he couldn't ask. Earlier, he'd suspected her of being a whore. Now it crossed his mind that perhaps she was a virgin.

"You go in." He handed her a candle and motioned to the door of his bedroom. "I'll douse the lamps and stoke the heater," he said.

He waited until the door closed behind her, then turned the wick down on the lamp and filled the wash basin with warm water from the kettle. In the dim glow, he shucked off his shirt, pants, woolen socks, and long underwear and swiftly, thoroughly, washed himself from top to toe. He'd shaved that morning, but now he drew the straight razor over his jaw and neck again.

It was a habit he'd grown away from since Molly's death, this ritual grooming every night before he went to bed. It was a legacy from his father.

Before his wedding to Molly, Zachary had talked with Noah about women and their ways, and part of his practical advice had been always to go to the marriage bed washed of sweat and clean shaven.

Unbidden came the image of Molly, wrapped in his arms, her nose buried in his neck, her shy whisper tickling his ear.

Dearest Noah, you always smell so good.

He thrust the memory away as he toweled himself dry, dumped the basin in the slop bucket, and after a moment's indecision, tugged his pants on again. He took a deep breath, willing his thoughts away from the quicksand of remembrance as he opened the bedroom door.

She was already in bed. Only the high, ruffled neckline of

her white flannel gown showed above the patchwork comforter. She tried for a smile when he came into the room but didn't quite succeed. After a single, startled glance at his uncovered chest with its mat of dark hair, she looked away.

He took the candle from the dresser and carried it to the small bench beside the bed. He blew it out, removed his pants, and climbed in naked under the covers. His weight made the mattress sag, bringing her closer toward him.

For long moments, he lay perfectly still, aware of her light breathing, the smell of the soap they'd both used, wondering if she could hear the way his heart was hammering against the wall of his chest. At last, he propped himself on an elbow and reached out and gently drew her closer, one hand on her shoulder, the other on a narrow flannel-covered hip.

She was trembling, and he was conscious of how delicate she was, how big he must seem to her.

"Are you afraid of me, Annie?" he whispered. "I won't hurt you, I promise."

"I—I've never done this before." Her choked whisper was so soft, he had to lean close to hear it.

"I'll try to make it as easy as I can for you." She didn't answer, and for long moments he stroked her shoulder and arm with his fingertips, and when she began to relax, he unfastened only the top buttons of her gown so he could slip his fingers in and touch the velvety skin of her neck.

Soft. She was so soft.   He'd *forgotten the delightful softness of a woman's body—Molly's body—*.

Ruthlessly, he slammed the top on the treacherous box of memory and nailed it tightly shut, forcing himself to think only of here and now.

This wasn't love, he reminded himself ruthlessly. This was seduction, but it wasn't love. As long as he kept them separate—

He bent down and put his mouth over hers in a light, feathery kiss. He took his time, savoring the sweet taste of her skin, the warmth and softness of her neck. Her lips were soft and full, closed until his tongue teased them open. Her breath, the taste of her mouth, was pleasing. He felt her catch her breath as the kiss deepened.

"You taste good," he murmured to her.

Tentatively, her chapped hand came up and lightly rested on his bare arm, and he could feel the tips of her small breasts against his chest, the supple and surprising strength of her long, narrow frame teasing him through the maddening fabric of her gown.

His starved body reacted with violence to her nearness. He drew back for a moment, regaining a shaky control.

"Can—can we take this off?" His voice was rough with passion. Before she could answer, he found the hem of the garment and pulled it up and over her head. She didn't resist.

He wished he'd left the candle lit so he could see her. Her skin was satin smooth. He groaned with impatience as his trembling hands learned the shape of her, the gentle curve of hip, the hollow of concave stomach, the slight swell of breasts. He took a tender nipple in his mouth and suckled it, and she gasped.

Pleasure knotted inside of him, a sweet delight.

"I'm not hurting you, am I, Annie?" His voice sounded strangled, and his breath was coming in short bursts, as if he'd been running.

"No. It doesn't hurt, it's—it's, ummmm, peculiar." It was little more than a breath of sound against his cheek.

Peculiar? He grinned and slid a hand down over her velvety stomach, his fingers discovering her silky mound. Soon she was hot, damp. With the last remnants of his control disappearing, he deftly positioned her beneath him, insinuating himself between her legs, trying not to hurry.

Her arms came around him, and her lips met his in shy, eager acceptance. She moved, clumsily, against him, and he gritted his teeth against the exquisite, driving urge to plunge into her.

He tried to make his entry smooth and slow, but the unbelievably hot, wet tightness of her passage combined with his own long abstinence undid him. At the last moment, when he knew without doubt that she was a virgin, he fought for control, but it was too late. With a strangled cry and an inner sense of despair at his impatience, he lunged, once, again, and at the final instant—

There must not be a child—there must never be a child of his again.

With superhuman effort, he pulled out of her, groaning as his seed spilled on her belly and legs and on the sheet beneath them.

He collapsed beside her, the swirling delight of release making his body seem boneless and light. In the aftermath of passion, he was ashamed of his haste.

"I'm sorry, Annie," he murmured. "Next time, it will be better for you, I promise." He gently disentangled their bodies and moved a careful distance away, so that no part of him touched her. Within moments, he slept.

Annie felt somehow bereft. She heard his breathing change, becoming deep and even. She waited until the pattern was well established before groping for her nightdress and struggling into it, careful to keep her movements from waking him, conscious of his warm, wet stickiness on her belly and legs.

She lay on her back, scrupulously keeping the distance he'd drawn between them. She'd always slept with her sister, and having this man beside her was going to take getting used to.

Her private parts throbbed with the strangest mixture of pain and thwarted pleasure. She stared wide-eyed into the darkness, confused and a little frightened by this act that had changed her from spinster to married woman.

Elinora had done her best to explain it. "It's either heaven or hell, dearie, depending on the man," her landlady had said, but this hadn't been either one. There must be something between the two extremes that Elinora hadn't told her, Annie deduced.

Would it be possible to ask in a letter? Elinora had told her to write about anything at all and promised to do her best to answer honestly.

Dear, forthright Elinora. Tears filled Annie's eyes as she thought of the countless miles that now separated her from her best and only friend. The night before her proxy wedding, Annie's rotund little landlady had brewed a pot of ginger tea and spoken candidly to her about this entire aspect of marriage.

"Some men are thoughtful, see. They try to pleasure their women. But there are others unskilled at such things, unaware, or just uncaring that women can enjoy the act as much as men. I was lucky in marrying Mr. Potts; he was one of the giving sort. I pray your Noah Ferguson is like him, pet."

Was he, Annie wondered? So far, Noah was a puzzle. One minute he was friendly, and the next there was this vast distance.

He'd been gentle at first, but then a madness she didn't wholly understand had taken him over. And just when the first, fierce pain inside her dwindled and another sensation began, he'd made that strangled sound and torn himself away and it was over.

At least she knew why he'd pulled back like that. Again,

Elinora had explained. "You know about babies, pet, and how they're made. A clever girl like you doesn't work with a hundred others and not come by that information," she'd begun, going on to explain to an astonished Annie how men and women prevented them.

She'd described the technique Noah had just used, but she'd advised Annie not to rely on her husband in this matter.

"Out in that wilderness, he's likely to want a passel of young 'uns, so don't count on him being any help," she'd warned Annie. "Farmers need a big family to help with the work. But a woman don't last long when she carries a baby every year. You have to take care of yourself in such things, my girl. There are female preventatives you can use to make sure one child's well grown before another's planted, and if you're clever, he don't ever need to know."

Annie had cringed at the thought of still another deception. She'd already told so many lies that she could hardly remember all of them, and preventing babies seemed so unnecessary.

"I *want* babies, Elinora," she'd protested. "I want lots of babies."

"More fool you," Elinora had snorted. "Wait until you know for certain what sort of man he really is." And so, in Annie's trunk, hidden among her petticoats, was the device Elinora had given her, a sponge with a string attached, and directions for a vinegar solution.

It didn't look as if she'd need to make use of it, however. If tonight was any indication, it seemed that Noah and Elinora were of one mind, whether they realized it or not. He wasn't taking any chance that she'd get with child, and it made her feel empty, diminished in some unexplainable fashion.

Gradually, Annie's weary body began to relax in the strange bed, beside the man who was now her husband in more than name.

Careful not to disturb him, she turned on her side and curled into a ball, sorely missing Bets's warm body close against her back.

A log fell in the heater, and outside the dog barked in response to a far-off, unearthly howling. Annie shivered, thinking of the miles of wilderness that surrounded this place, and how totally dependent she and Bets were on the strong man sleeping beside her.

She hated being dependent on anyone. She'd never felt as lonely in her entire life as she did at this moment, not even when her mother had died.

But she would get used to it, Annie told herself fiercely, trying to ignore the tears that trickled down her face and soaked the pillow. It was a chance for a different sort of life, the only chance she and her sister might ever have.

She'd gotten used to the factory, and she'd been only a little girl when she started there. She'd gotten used to taking care of her sick mother, to being solely responsible for Bets. She fished for her handkerchief, tucked under the pillow, and softly blew her nose.

She'd get used to this man. She'd get used to being his second wife, chosen not by love, but by necessity.

All she needed was time.

Chapter Five

March 26, 1886

Medicine Hat, Northwest Territories

Dear, dear Elinora,

Your first letter just reached me, and I'm so glad to have it, and am answering forthwith because I have many things to tell you and twice as many other troublesome matters for which I long for your assistance.

First, I shall try to answer your questions.

Yes, Bets is over the grippe, and although she still coughs a lot, she is much improved. As to the weather, there is still a great deal of snow on the ground, but some days are quite tolerable— one can now visit the outhouse without frostbite!

You ask about the view, and I have to smile. There's a great deal of nothing at all, empty, rolling plains and vast sky and precious few trees. As I'm sure I mentioned in my first letter, the ranch is situated only a short distance from the South Saskatchewan River, and Noah says there are willows along it which turn quite green in summer, but for now, everything is white, although sunrise and sunset are quite wonderful on days when the sky is clear.

As for me, my health is good, as always, but oh, my dear Elinora, sometimes (at least a dozen times each day) I fear I'm not suited to this ranching life at all.

My first week here, Noah took me outside to show me what "chores" would be mine, and for the first time in my entire life, I encountered cows and chickens and pigs and horses. I was, and am still, utterly terrified of all of them, although I do my best not to appear so to Noah. He seems to find my ignorance amusing, at least outdoors, and the surprising thing is that Bets doesn't share any of my concerns. She is quite at home around the animals in the barnyard. Noah has even promised to teach her to ride a horse when spring comes, and he's given her a kitten whom she's named Tar.

With me, it's quite a different story. He's trying to teach me to milk, but the cow hates me and either slaps me across the face with her tail or deliberately puts her filthy foot in the pail.

One rooster with a terrible disposition lies in wait to chase me, jumping on my back and pecking every time I step out the door, and I now carry an empty pail so that I can drop it over him, putting a heavy stone on top, thereby trapping him until Noah comes and sets him loose again. If only I had the stomach for it, I'd serve the beast up as Sunday dinner! (The rooster, not Noah.)

As for horses, I had no idea how large they are up close.

And pigs—dear Elinora, is it true they have a tendency to eat *their young, or is Noah having a joke at my expense? Jake, the old dog, is the only animal with whom I feel a true kinship.*

Inside the house, things are not a whole lot better. Because you took such fine care of us and I worked so many years in the factory, there's a great deal I don't know about housewifery. I feel the ghost of Noah's first wife watching me with disapproval as I dust her house and scrub her floors and try to cook on her stove. (That reminds me, do you have a reliable recipe for making bread? I've tried, but the results of my efforts are not edible, to say the least. Even the chickens refused the last attempt, and as you probably know, chickens eat anything at all.)

I know all too well that Noah compares me to that other wife and finds me wanting. Last week, I rearranged some small items on the sideboard, and although he didn't say anything, he soon put them all back just the way she must have had them.

Enough of this whining. There is also good news. Elinora, I can hardly believe it myself. You remember my last letter was filled with the difficulties of caring for Noah's father? Well, a near miracle has occurred, and it's thanks to Bets. She's befriended the old man and is teaching him her sign language, and his disposition is improved beyond belief now that he can communicate. The two of them have endless games of checkers, and Bets is always able to understand what he needs and wants.

Taken altogether, my dear friend, I have been more than fortunate with this "adventure," as you label it. Noah is the most generous of husbands. He took me to town last week and insisted I buy warmer clothing for Bets and for myself, and he eats whatever I prepare without complaint and thanks me politely for my attentions to his father. If at times lonely tears drip into the dishwater and I long for the kind of romance I used to moon over in my beloved dime novels, I remind myself that Noah could have been fat and ugly, with warts on his chin, a bulbous nose, and a mean nature.

Instead, as I told you, he actually resembles those

mythical old-fashioned heroes, tall and strong and handsome. And, unfortunately, silent most of the time. He's not a talker, and I needn't remind you, Elinora, that I am. He's kind, he's unfailingly polite, and he's unnaturally quiet. At times I even wish he'd lose his temper and rage at me, but he's far too controlled for such excess of emotion.

I can hear you telling me to count my blessings, and you're right, of course.

And now, enough of me. Are you well? Are the new girls behaving themselves? Is Fanny still with you? I know she doesn't read, or I would write to her. Give her my regards, and tell her that although I don't miss the factory, I do miss her.

I miss you too, dear Elinora, more than I can ever say. I feel so far away from you. I wonder, shall we ever again share a cup of tea and a wicked gossip?

Write soon. I love you.

Your old friend with a new name, Annie Ferguson.

April arrived.

The weather improved, and one windy day in midmonth, Annie awoke with laundry on her mind. Blankets, sheets, curtains, clothing; she suddenly wanted everything clean for spring.

"After breakfast I'll need your help in getting your father up, Noah," she announced as soon as she opened her eyes. "So I can change those filthy sheets on his bed. I need to do a big wash. Could you help me bring water in from the well to fill the copper washtubs and set them to heating?" Inspired, she added, "Also, Mr. Ferguson sorely needs a bath, and he could also do with a haircut and a shave."

It was the beginning of a long, hard, satisfying day.

Alone in the bedroom late that night, Annie sank deeper into the old tin tub, letting the hot, soapy water soothe the ache in her arms and shoulders and ease the tension in her back from bending over a washboard hour after hour.

Ooohhh, this was heaven.

Her hands were raw from scrubbing, and the entire house smelled of soap powder and garments fresh from the clothesline.

Weary as she was, there was an enormous sense of accomplishment in what she'd done today. For once, everything had gone perfectly.

Every sheet, every towel, every sock in the house was clean and dry and folded. Next door, Zachary Ferguson slept in a fresh and sweet-smelling bed. He was bathed, shaved, trimmed, and wearing a fresh nightshirt, and he looked a different man.

She'd said as much to Noah and gotten a quiet nod in return.

There was a tap at the door, and she jerked upright in the tub and then hurriedly ducked beneath the suds again as Noah came into the room, carrying a kettle. The candle on the dresser flickered as the door closed behind him, sending long shadows up the walls. He towered over her, and instinctively she folded her arms across her naked breasts. She was still shy about having him see her unclothed.

"I thought you could do with some more hot water," he said matter of factly. "Pull your feet back and I'll pour it in."

She'd never felt as exposed in her life. She could feel her whole upper body flushing as she curled her legs up and he slowly poured the steaming water into the tub.

"Thank you," she said weakly, waiting for him to go back into the other room.

But he stayed, looking down at her with such raw, kindling passion in his dark eyes that her heart began to hammer against her ribs and her breath caught in her throat. Slowly, daringly, she let her arms fall into the water, leaving her pink-tipped breasts exposed to his view.

"I thought maybe you'd let me wash your back," he said, and now there was no coolness in his voice. Indeed, its rough warmth seemed to stroke over Annie's bare skin, leaving a tingling trail of anticipation in its wake.

She gave a tremulous nod, and deliberately, never taking his eyes from her, he rolled his sleeves up past the elbow and knelt on the braided rug.

Noah lathered the cloth. He started slowly, at her neck, where tendrils of curly red hair were escaping the untidy bun on the top of her head. Her skin was gold-tinged in the candlelight, the back of her neck as fragile as a flower stalk.

Damn it all. He'd struggled with himself, trying to resist her these past weeks. He didn't want to desire her the way he did; he didn't want the thought of her to haunt him every waking moment. She wasn't the woman he loved, but he was forced to admit she was a woman he desired, a woman who intrigued and amused him with her quick-witted remarks, her contagious giggle, her endless energy and enthusiasm.

Why couldn't she have been older, colder, fatter, less appealing? Why couldn't she be more like the stolid person he'd envisioned when he wrote that confounded advertisement and mailed it to the paper?

He drew the washrag down, his eyes registering the slender curve of shoulder, waist, hip, his body reacting with fierce need, against his will, to the look and smell and feel of her.

She smelled of soap and of some other essence that was singularly her own, that he'd come to recognize, a musky, warm odor that inflamed his senses.

"Ohhh, that feels so good, Noah. Do it again, please."

He was trembling as he rinsed the cloth, soaped it again, and resumed the long, sensual stroking. This time, his hand slid around to cup her small breast, and the nipple rose hard against his palm.

He groaned and lost whatever battle he was fighting.

"Annie." The word was wrung out of him, low and tortured.

He slid his hands under her arms, and in one smooth motion lifted her dripping from the tub. She made a small, startled sound and he gave her a rueful grin.

"I do believe you're quite clean enough," he said with a catch in his voice, snatching up the towel from a nearby chair and wrapping her in it, blotting her dry, loosening it to dab gently at a shoulder, a narrow hip, a long stretch of thigh.

He scooped her up and laid her on the bed. It was cool in the room, and he covered her naked form with the quilt until his own clothes were off and he could slide under the sheets.

The first contact with her warm, damp nakedness made him shudder. He gathered her close, wrapping his arms and legs around her, drunk with the feeling of skin against skin. He took her head in his hands and held it, kissing her lips and the long line of her throat, taking first one nipple and then the next into his mouth, moving down the satiny, narrow ribcage, nipping at prominent hipbones until at last his mouth found her center.

"Noah!" There was both shock and pleasure in her protest.

When she overcame shyness and relaxed, her body began to move instinctively, in a rhythm impossible for him to mistake. The small, desperate sounds she was making were more than he could bear. He slid up and in one long, steady motion, he entered her, half mad with wanting, but mindful that he mustn't hurt her.

Long, careful moments later, she exploded beneath him in a paroxysm of delight, and he muffled her cries with his mouth, delight taking hold of him until he lost all control.

His seed spilled and spilled, and he was too far beyond thought to pull away. She fell asleep in his arms and didn't wake when he gently untangled himself and got up to blow out the candle.

When he lay down beside her again, he made certain her bare shoulders were well covered, but he moved until there was the usual distance between them so that no part of her warm body was near enough to touch him.

* * *

In the darkness, she awakened from a dream, knowing that she was falling in love with Noah.

His lovemaking had changed her, and she knew that her perceptions of herself were forever altered. Her body had depths and needs she'd never suspected, and in her heart was amazement and tenderness, gratitude to the husband who'd taught her these mysterious truths about herself.

But instead of lying warm in his embrace, she was facing his back. She slid one tentative arm up and around him, snuggling close and curling herself like a spoon to fit his sleeping shape.

He wasn't asleep. His body stiffened in her embrace, and after a moment he carefully lifted her arm and moved as far away as the bed would allow.

Annie's body stiffened with hurt. She swallowed, her face and body burning with humiliation. She stared into the darkness, fighting the tears that threatened.

It hurt. It hurt more than she would have believed

possible, this constant, quiet rejection of her love. It told her more plainly than any words that Noah might succumb to the desires of his body—he'd even make very certain she, too, enjoyed the marriage bed—but anything beyond that coupling was not allowed between them.

Companionship, laughter, conversation, the elements she instinctively knew constituted deep and abiding love, those were things Noah was unwilling to share with her. Those were the things he'd shared with his Molly, and he guarded them jealously.

It felt to Annie as though the ghost woman of that first marriage even shared the bed now, lying between herself and Noah.

With one silent gesture, he'd made it clear that the wall he maintained around himself and his deepest feelings was firmly in place, and that although his body might succumb to Annie, his heart would belong always to Molly.

Was this, too, something that she'd get used to as time passed? As the slow, dark minutes of that night dragged into hours, and the beginnings of a new day drew closer, she could only pray that it might be so.

Chapter Six

It snowed again the following day, and it wasn't until early May that the mud began to dry and the first faint tinge of green appeared on the prairie.

Noah had gone to mend fences right after breakfast one sunny morning, and Annie, still unable to bake a loaf of bread that resembled anything but a rock, made up her mind once and for all that they'd just have to learn to live on biscuits forevermore.

She'd just taken a batch of popovers from the oven when Jake's frantic barking announced visitors.

"Hello, neighbor." Gladys Hopkins greeted Annie with a warm handshake and a wide smile, handing her a loaf of fresh bread as high as a haystack and a jar of dark red preserves.

"Set the dough last night, baked it first thing. That's some wild strawberry jam to go with. This here's my daughter Rose. She's been just dying to meet your little sister. She's been at me every day to come over, but we had to wait for the weather. Now where is that sister of yours? Feeling better than when she first arrived, I hope?"

"Bets is very well, thanks, Gladys. Pleased to meet you.

Rose." Annie smiled at the plump little girl whose golden hair hung in careful ringlets down her back.

Annie was uncomfortably aware that neither Rose nor Gladys knew as yet that her sister was deaf.

"Bets is having a game of checkers with Mr. Ferguson. I'll get her." Annie, feeling flustered and more than a little apprehensive, hurried into Zachary's bedroom and signed to her sister and the old man that they had company. Neither was particularly pleased at the news—Betsy's face became anxious at the ordeal of meeting strangers, and Zachary scowled and slumped dejectedly into the pillows at this interruption.

Bets and Zachary had become the best of companions in the past weeks. By now there was a powerful bond between the young girl whose ears didn't work and the old man who'd lost the ability to speak.

Taking Bets's hand, Annie led her out and introduced her, adding an explanation of Bets's handicap as matter-of-factly as she could.

"She's—she's deef and dumb?" Gladys's eyes seemed almost to be popping out of her head as she studied Bets. "I never had the foggiest idea she was deaf and dumb."

"Deaf," Annie corrected firmly. "But she's certainly not dumb. Bets talks, but she does it with her hands. She'll be glad to show Rose how."

Rose was half hidden behind her mother's skirts, peering out at Bets as though expecting her to suddenly foam at the mouth or grow horns.

The violent hammering of Zachary's cane on the floor made them all jump, and Annie realized how seldom he'd banged it recently.

Bets felt the vibration, picked up her skirt, and flew in to see what he wanted. Annie knew the girl was relieved to escape the scrutiny of the Hopkins women.

Gladys whispered, "Ain't you scared he'll hammer her with that thing?"

Annie laughed and shook her head. "Those two are thick as thieves," she assured Gladys. "See, Bets has taught Mr. Ferguson to sign, and it's made the world of difference to him. He can let us know what he wants now, and he's much happier. Bets is awfully fond of him. He's like a grandpa to her. Come and sit and have some coffee, won't you?"

Annie sliced Gladys's bread, envious of the yeasty loaf. She put out some of her own popovers and set the butter crock and the preserves on the table.

Rose, with a dejected expression, slumped down across the table from the women, obviously prepared to be bored to death.

"Rose, would you be kind enough to take this bread and some coffee in to Mr. Ferguson?" Annie spread jam on a thick slice and thrust the plate and cup at the girl before she could refuse. "And then ask Bets to show you her cat. There's a new litter of kittens out in the shed, too. She'll take you to see them."

"But—but how can I ask her anything if she can't—" Rose's voice trailed off at a look from her mother.

"She can read a lot of what you say on your lips," Annie reassured her gently. "Just try."

Rose reluctantly did as she was asked. In a moment, she and Bets went silently out to the shed where the kittens were, and just as Annie hoped, it wasn't long before the two girls had brought the entire litter of kittens inside and were giggling together at their antics. Bets showed Rose her sign for cats, and slowly the two began to communicate.

Gladys watched them and then turned to Annie with a shamefaced expression. "You must excuse us dearie. We don't mean no offense. It's just we ain't never seen a deaf and—a deef young'un before," she amended hastily. "How did she come to be that way?"

Annie explained, and in the process revealed a great deal of her and Betsy's background.

In turn Gladys told of coming in a covered wagon to Canada from Minnesota with her husband, Harold, where she was pregnant with Rose. Some of the light weny out of her blue eyes and tears welled up when she confided that she'd lost three babies in succession after Rose was born.

"Looks like she'll be our only one," she said with a sigh. "It's a shame. My Harold would have liked a big family." She took a sip of her coffee and lathered her own preserves on one of Annie's biscuits, lowering her voice so Rose wouldn't hear.

"Easy for men to want more, ain't it? They don't go through it all. Why, I remember Noah sayin' hi wanted a dozen more babies when Jeremy was born and the look on poor Molly's face—"

She stopped suddenly, and her already rosy face turned magenta. "Oh, my. I am sorry. Me and my big mouth." She rammed the entire biscuit in and chewed ferociously, as if to prevent any further in discretion.

Noah wanted a dozen more babies.

Annie felt as if she'd been hit in the stomach. She thought of the nights when he made love to her—nearly ever night, now—and of how careful he was to pull away from her body so that there'd be no babies.

Only that once had he ever lost control.

To hide the pain that she knew was mirrored on her face, she got up and shoved more wood into the stove and filled their cups again with fresh coffee, coming to a decision.

Better the ghost you know.

When she sat down, she leaned across and put her chapped hand on Gladys's arm. "Gladys, I need a favor. I need you to tell me about Molly, please. Noah won't so much as say her name, and I need to know what kind of woman she was." She gestured at the room. "Every single thing here is hers. It feels like I'm living with a spirit I never even met."

Gladys looked uncertain. "Oh, I don't know. You sure it won't bother you none, hearin' about Noah's first wife?"

Doing the best acting job of her life, Annie shook her head vehemently and plastered on a smile. "Of course not. How silly. What did she look like?"

Gladys looked over her shoulder as if expecting Molly to materialize. Then she leaned forward in a confiding manner, resting her elbows on the table, her voice little more than a whisper. "Well, let's see. Molly was lots shorter than you are, and she—" Gladys made a motion that indicated Molly had possessed a good-sized bosom, narrow waist, and shapely hips. "She was real womanly," Gladys said discreetly.

Annie crossed her arms over her own meager bosom. Even though every single syllable Gladys uttered was a knife in her heart, she nodded encouragement and fixed the smile on her lips.

"She had pale, smooth hair, sorta like flax, long and braided up around her head like a crown. She had these dark blue eyes, and oh, my, she was so sweet. Gentle and sort of quiet. She had a real nice way with her, did Molly. And she could turn her hand to anything. Why, her piecrust was the best I've ever eaten."

The eulogy went on and on, and Annie died by degrees, her smile feeling more and more like a grimace.

"How—how did Noah meet her, Gladys?"

"Oh, they lived in the Hat, her and her papa. Molly's father was a fine man, a preacher. When his wife died back east, he came out west here to the prairies. Molly was just seventeen. He set up the first church in Medicine Hat. Poor man, he died last year himself. It was his heart, but folks believe it was losing his daughter and grandson the way he did." She shook her head. "It hit us all right hard when he passed away. He was well liked by all that knew him."

Annie thought of her own drunken father and shivered.

It didn't seem fair at all. It was as if the fates were playing a joke on her, sending her here to be Noah's second wife.

If Annie had set her mind to imagining her own exact opposite, she supposed that Molly would have been that image. And guess who any man in his right mind would choose, given a choice? she thought bitterly.

No wonder Noah loved Molly still, with no room left over in his heart for Annie.

Chapter Seven

By mid-June, summer had come to the prairies.

One afternoon Annie looked at Bets and saw that she was blooming like one of the wild roses she'd just picked and put in a jar on the table. The good food and clean air had done exactly what Annie had prayed they would. The cough that had plagued Bets for more than two years was gone, and her painfully thin body was showing the first timid signs of a bosom and hips.

It was a busy time on the farm. Calves were being born, Noah was finishing the last of the spring planting, the early lettuce and radishes Annie had planted in the garden at the back of the house were up, and the kitchen door stood open to catch the fragrant evening breeze.

Annie drew in deep draughts of the warm, fresh air and prayed that she wouldn't throw up again.

"What is wrong with you?" Bets's hands flew, her brow furrowed with worry over her big sister. "Everyday, sick, sick, all the time. Maybe you go to see doctor, yes? I worry over you," she added plaintively, wrapping her arms around Annie. "I love you," she added, pulling away enough so Annie could see the sign.

"I love you too." Annie returned the hug, fighting against the nausea that made her stomach churn. She was in the midst of making supper, and she'd had to run to the shed twice in the past hour.

It was a time of new beginnings, and for the past week, Annie had been fairly certain she was pregnant.

It had taken her a while to figure out what was wrong with her. What had confused her was that Elinora had written that the natural order of such things was to be sick in the morning and miss her monthly.

Instead, Annie had been fine every morning and miserably sick in the afternoons. Her monthly came for a day and went away, came for another and went away, in fits and starts.

She was going to have to tell Noah. Her hands knotted into fists. How would he react when he found out?

The thought of telling him weighed heavily on her. Not that she feared his temper, although she knew he had one. She'd seen him furiously angry at times, when a renegade wolf killed one of the best milk cows, and when the Medicine Hat Times reported some new insanity the politicians had decreed law.

She'd also witnessed the gentleness in him, with a sick newborn calf, and always with her sister. From the very first, he'd made a real effort to learn Bets's sign language. And with his father, Noah was unfailingly thoughtful and kind.

Annie knew also the depths of his passion and the intensity of his loving; not once had he taken her without thought of her pleasure. Indeed, he'd taught her to want him, to need as terribly as he that physical joining.

But he'd been most deliberate about preventing babies. Without ever saying a word, he made it clear each time they loved that he absolutely didn't want a child with her.

Well, he was about to have one anyway, Annie thought rebelliously, slamming down the oven door and reaching inside, forgetting that the towel she used as a potholder was threadbare.

"Owww! Lordie, owww!" She howled with pain and dropped the pot, spilling the entire stew all over the oven door and the floor. Noah would be in for his supper in a few moments, and now the meal was ruined.

Spill the stew, ruin the bread, get herself with child; couldn't she do anything right? Annie threw herself into a chair, put her head down on her arms, and burst into a storm of tears.

Bets patted her back and then quietly cleaned up the mess, wisely letting Annie cry for a while. Then the young girl made a vinegar poultice for Annie's burned fingers, brewed a pot of tea, poured two cups, and indicated that Annie should take one to Zachary.

"You go talk with Mr. Ferguson. I will make us eggs and bacon for dinner," she promised.

"There's no bread," Annie said miserably. "Today's batch was so bad I took it out and buried it behind the bam."

"I will make biscuits," Bets assured her. "Go, go." She pointed towards Zachary's room.

Well, the biscuits her little sister made would be lighter than hers, that was certain, Annie concluded dolefully as she blew her nose and made her way in to sit beside Zachary.

Zachary looked at her and gave her his crooked smile, and Annie did her best to return it. How strange it was that the old man who'd scared her half to death at first had become someone she liked to be with. She and Bets and Zachary had spent delightful moments together in the past months.

In short spurts, using his garbled speech and a lot of sign

language, he'd laboriously told the sisters tales of his early life in eastern Canada, of how after his beloved Mary died, he and Noah, a young man by that time, had emigrated to the western plains and found this place on the South Saskatchewan River, building the cabin that eventually became this house and slowly building up their herd of cattle. He told of renegade Indians and drunken white men who'd threatened the Fergusons' very existence here, and of how he and Noah together had fought them off and won.

Listening, Annie had gained a greater understanding of Noah, of his quiet strength, his courage, the steely determination that made him the man he was.

The man she'd fallen in love with, she thought despairingly as she handed Zachary his tea and lowered herself wearily into the rocking chair Bets had moved beside his bed.

Lordie, why couldn't she have settled for just *liking* the man she'd married? Why in heaven did she have to *love* him to distraction?

Annie tilted her head back and closed her eyes. There were times when she could pretend that Noah loved her back, those rare moments when he smiled at her with affection, or walked with her along the river bank in the evening when they talked together of the day's happenings. And there were the nights, especially the nights, when he made such passionate love to her. But each time, afterwards, the distancing came again, the drawing away.

A sound from Zachary made her open her eyes. He was watching her, and the part of his face not affected by the paralysis was smiling, his dark eyes, so like Noah's, gentle and questioning.

"Tired?" His hand moved in question. He gestured at the burns on her palms. "Sore?"

"I spilled the damn stew all over the floor and burned my hands in the bargain." She tried for a smile, but the tears welled up again and rolled down her cheeks, and despair overwhelmed her.

"Oh, Zachary," she wailed. "Why can't I do anything right?" The words tumbled out of their own accord. "The bread I make is like rock, my piecrust isn't fit to eat, I burned that confounded roast last week to a cinder and—and now—" The words welled up in her and she couldn't stop them. "Oh, Zachary, I'm—I'm going to have a—a baby, and Noah—he doesn't—doesn't want babies." Tears dripped off her chin and wet the front of her dress.

Zachary groped under his pillow and handed her the clean handkerchief that Bets put there each morning.

"You want me to talk to Noah?" he asked.

Alarmed, Annie shook her head, mopped at her eyes, and tried to stop sobbing. She blew her nose hard and gulped. "No, thank you. I—I absolutely must tell him myself."

"He's a good man," Zachary signed with a sigh. "He loved his little son with all his heart."

"I know that. And I know he loved Molly that way too, and that he still misses her, and—and Jeremy, too."

Zachary nodded, his own sorrow for his lost grandson plain on his face.

"But that's over, Zachary. They're dead and gone, and nothing can bring them back." Her voice became passionate, and all the feelings she'd stifled for so long came pouring out in a torrent of words. "I want him to be happy about *my* baby, I want him to love *this* baby and not always just brood over what he's lost," Annie went on, her voice filled with anger, not even caring that she was almost shouting. "So what if what Gladys said was right and his blessed Molly was perfect and I'm— I'm not? This baby"—her hands cupped her still- flat abdomen—"this baby deserves a father just as much as Jeremy ever did. It's not my fault that Molly and Jeremy died, this new baby shouldn't have to pay just because—"

"That's quite enough."

Annie jumped and almost fell off her chair as Noah's voice thundered from directly behind her. She whirled to face him, feeling the blood drain out of her extremities, wondering how in heaven he'd managed to come in without her hearing him.

And Lord, how long had he been listening? He was in his stockinged feet; he must have taken off his muddy boots outside, and of course she'd forgotten the kitchen door was wide open.

Speechless now, she stared at him in horror, knowing that the guilt she felt was plainly written on her face. "Noah, I didn't mean—"

"Come with me." He reached down with both hands and grasped her arms, his fingers like iron bands digging into her flesh, almost lifting her off her feet.

In a moment they were in their own bedroom, and Noah had slammed the door shut so hard that it seemed the whole house shook.

Annie's knees were trembling, along with the rest of her. She whirled to face him when he released her arm.

Her breath caught at the fury on his face. His strong features were cold and hard, his jaw clenched with rage. His narrowed eyes weren't cold, however; they were like black pools of fire. He glared at her, and she felt as if his gaze had the power to sear her. His hands were planted low on his hips, and she could see that his huge fists were clenched tight enough to turn the knuckles white.

"Noah," she began in a shaky voice. "I'm sorry, I never meant for you to hear—"

"To hear what?" he interrupted, his voice choked with fury. "To hear how you talk when my back's turned? To find out you're having a baby"—the word came out as a sneer—"and that I'm the last to know, after you've told my father and your sister and that Elinora woman you write to, and probably Gladys Hopkins, who'll delight in informing the whole of Medicine Hat?"

"Oh, phooey, I did not tell Bets or Gladys," she denied hotly, refusing to let him see that he frightened her. She plopped down on the bed before her legs gave out. "I didn't mean to tell your father, but I burned myself and ruined dinner and somehow it just came out. I *said* I was sorry." She swallowed back the nausea that rose in her throat.

"You will *never*"—his words were measured and he spoke very low, almost in a whisper—*"never* again speak of Molly or of Jeremy. Never, do you hear? They are not your business. They have nothing whatsoever to do with you. You didn't know them, and I will not have you tarnishing their memory."

Her mouth fell open and she gaped at him. *"Me?* Tarnish the memory of your first wife and child? How can you say such a thing?" The unfairness of the accusation overwhelmed her.

"And as for the unfortunate child you carry," he went on as if she hadn't spoken, "I wish to God it were otherwise. I wish it had never happened, but the blame is mine as much as your own, and I will do my duty by him, just as I have with you."

Unfortunate child? Duty?

In an instant, all Annie's remorse turned to outrage.

"Your—your duty?" she sputtered. "You—you pompous hypocrite, you. Is *duty* what you call what goes on in this bed, then?" She thumped the bedcovers with both her doubled-up fists and sprang to her feet so he couldn't look down on her.

"It was more than duty that started this baby, Noah, whatever you choose to believe." She spat the words at him and met his eyes fearlessly now, her chin held high. "You cling to the past as if your dead wife and child hold all the love and happiness life will ever offer you, and I'm sorry for you, because you can't see what's right under your nose. When I lie with you, I feel much more than duty."

She struggled to keep her voice from trembling and failed. "God help me, I feel love for you, Noah Ferguson."

Chapter Eight

Annie could see some of Noah's righteous anger giving way to shocked disbelief.

"And as for the child," she went on, "the only thing unfortunate about our baby is that his father doesn't want him. Well, I'll make up for that, never fear, because already I love him with my whole heart and soul." She'd made it through without crying, and she was proud of that. But the turmoil in her stomach made the victory short-lived. She gagged suddenly, pressed a hand over her mouth, and ran as fast as she could for the outhouse.

Noah didn't move. Annie's words were like blows from a heavy fist that stunned him and held him immobile.

She'd said that she loved him.

Pain wrenched at his gut. He didn't want her love, he told himself savagely. He didn't want to love her back, or care for the child he'd carelessly allowed to begin. He *couldn't* give that kind of love again, didn't she see that?

Sweat broke out on his forehead, and he shut his eyes tight, willing himself to remember.

For weeks now, he'd struggled to recall the exact shape of

Molly's face, the precise sound of his son's baby voice calling him daddy. They were recollections Noah had believed to be engraved on his very soul, impossible ever to erase.

But fight it as he would, Noah's memories of them were fading. Now, in his dreams, it was more often than not Annie's husky voice he heard instead of Molly's softer, sweeter tones, and God knew that when he held Annie in his arms, in this room, in this bed, the sweet passion he'd awakened in her and the mad, bottomless hunger she stirred in him left no room for memories or thoughts of another.

Because, some traitorous part of him whispered, with Molly there had never been the sexual intensity he experienced with Annie. And he felt the foulest sort of traitor to acknowledge that there were days—even weeks—now, when he didn't think of his first wife at all.

The rest of June passed with excessive politeness and long silences between them.

July brought blistering heat and long hours of backbreaking work for Noah, and for Annie as well. Days started at four and ended only at full dark.

The words they'd hurled at each other remained between them.

In bed, they lay rigidly back to back, each achingly aware of the other's body, each longing for the love-making that had been their only meeting place. Feeling wretched, neither reached out for the other.

Annie, wounded by his rejection, couldn't, and Noah, wanting her more with every sultry, wasted night, wouldn't.

"Bets, I'll take the lunch out to Noah today." It was nearing the end of August, and he was clearing land that bordered the river, about a mile away from the house.

Annie usually sent Bets out with Noah's lunch every afternoon, but today she'd been busy making rhubarb jam all morning, and she was hot and thoroughly sick of being indoors.

The jam had turned out, though. She could hardly believe how impressive the row of jars with their pink contents looked lined up on the table. Even more amazing, she'd made good bread four times now, tall, golden loaves, crusty and delicious.

It was the most peculiar thing. She'd waited until Noah was out one day and then, feeling both guilty and defiant, she had ventured up to the attic to look at the beautifully carved cradle, setting it to rocking and wondering if the child she carried would ever sleep in it.

There, in a box behind the cradle, she'd found recipes that Molly must have written. Feeling like a thief in her own home, Annie brought them down and began trying them.

Unlike the ones Elinora had sent, these were easy to follow, and one after the other, she turned out perfect bread, piecrust, puddings, even a sponge cake.

And for the first time, Annie found herself whispering fervent *thank-yous* to the ghost who shared her house.

Exuberant with the success of the jam, she relished the long walk along the riverbank and through the fields to where Noah was working.

She saw him from a distance, using the team of heavy workhorses, Buck and Bright, to pull stumps.

His snug-fitting pants were tucked into high leather boots, and he'd taken his blue shirt off and hung it on a nearby bush. Brown suspenders rested on equally brown-bare skin, and he had a wide-brimmed straw hat on his head. The muscles in his arms and back bulged as he added his considerable strength to the efforts of the animals.

He didn't see her at first, and Annie's eyes traveled over his long, broad-shouldered body, sweat-sheened and powerful.

He was a beautiful-looking man. He was a man any

woman would be proud to claim as her husband.

Slowly, torturously, the gigantic stump parted from the earth, and Noah threw his fists to the sky and hollered in triumph, unaware that she was watching.

It was a revelation to see him this way, exhilarated and noisy. "Hello, Noah. I brought you fresh water and some sandwiches," she called as she walked across the torn earth to hand him the bucket she'd packed the lunch in.

He actually smiled at her. His face was streaked with dirt, and sweat poured from him.

"Thanks, Annie. Whew, it's a scorcher today. I'm thirsty and hungry both." He took his hat off and mopped his face with a red checkered bandanna. "There's a shady spot over by the riverbank." He paused, and she could tell he was uncertain as he added, "Will you come sit and share this with me?"

Annie hadn't planned to linger, but for the first time since their quarrel, the tension between them seemed somewhat eased.

"I'd like that, Noah." She didn't know about him, but she was sick and tired of the strain between them. She'd never been good at holding grudges. What purpose did they serve? Life went right on.

Besides, the thought of sitting somewhere cool for a spell was appealing. Her dress was light cotton, but her long skirts were cumbersome. She'd shoved her sunbonnet back, and as usual curls had escaped from under her sunbonnet and were glued to her forehead and neck with sweat. A fresh crop of freckles were undoubtedly popping out like gooseberries on her nose and cheeks, and she didn't care.

Noah retrieved his shirt and handed it to her to carry while he took the team down to the water for a drink and then turned them free to graze. When they were settled, he led the way to a sheltered, grassy knoll among the willows that bordered the riverbank.

Annie plunked herself down, relishing the feel of the cool grass. A slight breeze came drifting from the water. Meadowlarks trilled from the bushes.

Noah sat down beside her and opened the fresh tea towel she'd wrapped around his sandwiches and held them out to her.

Good thing she'd packed extra. She accepted a thick chicken sandwich. She seemed always to be starving these days. The early sickness had passed, leaving a bottomless hunger in its place.

Her belly had begun to gently round, but she was also putting on extra weight all over her body, the first time in her life that she'd been more than skin and bone.

"I made a dozen jars of rhubarb jam, and they turned out," she remarked, still feeling pleased with herself.

"This bread is delicious, too, Annie." He bit into another sandwich and chewed appreciatively.

"I guess I've finally gotten the knack."

"I guess the chickens are relieved," he said, and Annie blinked.

Was Noah actually joking with her?

She looked at him, and he was grinning. Another moment, and they were laughing together, the memory of her calamitous efforts at bread making forming a bond between them.

They finished the lunch, munching on apples and chatting easily now about the field he was clearing, the new colt that had been born the week before, the latest gossip in the Medicine Hat Times.

It was growing even hotter. Annie fanned herself with the dish towel, looking at the water, and an irresistible idea began to form.

"I'm going wading." She sat up and began unlacing her boots.

Noah nodded in agreement. "Why not come for a swim? It's hot enough to melt bullets, and there's a backwater down there just made for swimming. "

He stood and, without any hesitation, swiftly removed his boots, pants, and under drawers. Pretending to be oblivious to her startled gaze, he calmly walked down the embankment stark naked and dove straight in, disappearing entirely for a heart-stopping moment before he surfaced a short distance away from the shore.

"It's fine," he hollered, sending droplets flying as he shook water out of his ears. "It's cool. Come on in."

She hesitated for only a split second. Then a kind of madness seized her. She shucked off her dress and stockings, her long petticoat, until all that was left was her white cotton chemise and under drawers. She picked her way gingerly down to the water, aware that Noah, neck deep, was watching her every move.

The delicious coolness on her toes enchanted her. In a moment, she was up to her knees, and then her thighs.

"You tricked me," she gasped. "It's not just cool, it's downright freezing."

"Careful, the bottom drops off fast right about there." Noah swam over and stood, taking both of her hands in his.

"Can you swim, Annie?" Drops of water clung to his eyelashes, the whorls of dark hair on his chest glistened, and he smiled at her, lighthearted, boyish--and very bare.

The shock of the water and the sight of Noah's naked body was taking her breath away. "No, I can't swim," she gasped, clinging tight to his hands, laughing with the wonder of it all. "I've never done this before."

"Put your arms around my neck, but don't choke off my

air."

He turned his back to her and she looped her arms around him, heart hammering at the feel of his skin against hers, and in one smooth movement, he sank down into the water with her half floating on his back.

She screamed in delight as the chill of the water reached her buttocks, her back, her breasts. She clung to him, laughing uncontrollably, drunk with the sensation of weightlessness, the naked male body pressing against her. He swam a few strokes, and she felt the power of his muscles as he stroked and kicked, easily supporting her.

Like carefree children, they splashed and teased and played, until all at once, laughing up at him in waist deep water, Annie met his eyes and caught her breath.

The game had changed.

His arms slid further around her, and one hand cupped her breast. His mouth came down to claim hers, and with a groan, he scooped her up in his arms and carried her out of the water, up the bank to where the grass was soft.

He stripped her of dripping chemise and drawers, spread his shirt, and drew her down upon it.

Their loving was both easy and intense, because in this one thing they seemed to know instinctively what the other required.

The sun beat down upon them, the meadowlarks sang, and the rushing of the river muffled the sounds they made.

"I've lost my hairpins, and I can't put my hair back up without them." Annie was searching the grass.

Noah, dressed again in trousers and the crumpled blue shirt they'd lain on, knelt obligingly beside her and combed the ground in search of them.

"Here's three, is that enough?" He couldn't help but grin at the picture she made kneeling there in disarray, scowling as she tried to control the wild red curls covering her shoulders and tumbling down her back. Her freckled face was golden from the sun, her body voluptuous.

He refused to dwell on the reason for that new lushness, the child that grew within her. Today he was at peace, with her and with himself. There'd be time later to come to terms with the child.

"Thank you, Noah." She stuck the pins in her mouth and smiled at him as she wrestled with her unruly hair.

Her eyes were as green as the grass they knelt on, as wide and clear as the pool where they'd been swimming. He leaned forward and pressed a kiss on her swollen lips, then regretted his impetuous gesture when her eyes shimmered with sudden tears.

But she gave him a wide smile and pulled her stockings up, teasing him with one last glimpse of shapely leg before she struggled to her feet.

"I have to get back. Bets and Zachary will think I've been taken by Indians. Do I look decent again?"

He pretended to study her. Her dress was creased beyond redemption, and there was grass in her hair. He reached over and took it out before she tied the sunbonnet on.

"You look just fine," he assured her, knowing that anyone with half an eye could tell by the rich color in her cheeks and the slumberous look in her eyes that she'd been well and truly loved.

But Bets was too young and innocent for such thoughts, and if Zachary should notice, well, Zachary would be overjoyed that the strain of the past weeks was over and done with.

"Let the past go," he'd communicated to Noah just the other night. Zachary had come to love Annie, and he made no secret that he blamed Noah for the problems between them.

Yes, his father would be delighted to see Annie like this.

Noah tucked the dish towel into the lunch pail and handed it to her, and he watched as she set off across the field. A hundred yards off she turned and waved, and he raised a hand in response, feeling happy and more at peace than he'd been in a long while.

She disappeared over the hill, and he walked toward the peacefully grazing horses. "C'mon, boys. Buck, Bright, time to get back to work."

He was whistling as he harnessed them and led them over to another stump, and he was still whistling half an hour later when he heard the frantic call.

"Noah—Noah."

His body stiffened as he caught sight of Annie and Bets, skirts held high, racing towards him over the uneven ground.

A terrible foreboding filled him as he ran to meet them.

Chapter Nine

Bets was sobbing, her face soaked with tears and sweat. Annie, too, was crying as Noah reached them, her flushed face contorted into lines of anguish.

"What is it? What's happened?" He grasped Annie by the shoulders. "Tell me, for God's sake."

"It's—it's Zachary. Bets was—she was coming—to get us," she gasped. "I met her on the trail, I ran back to the house with her, but it—it was too late. Oh, Noah—" She gulped and her voice broke. "He's gone. Zachary's dead." She pressed her hands against her mouth, trying to still the sobs so she could talk.

"Bets said she—she was playing checkers with him, and he had some sort of a seizure, just for a moment or two, and then—then he just fell back on the pillows—"

An absolute stillness seemed to surround Noah. He heard the words, but they came from a great distance. He turned and ran over to unhook the team. Then, with his hand on the harness, he paused and laid his forehead against Buck's rough, warm flank.

His father was dead.

Hurrying served no purpose, because Zachary was no longer there for him, the way he'd been through the whole of Noah's life.

His wife, his child, and now his father. Fate had a way of taking everything he cared about. It was a reminder, a grim warning, not ever to let himself love without reservation.

November 14, 1886

My dear Elinora,

We're having the first real snowfall of the year, and it's still coming down like big, soft feathers. It's pretty, but it also makes me feel lonely and rather a prisoner. It's been over two months now, but Bets and I still can't seem to get through a day without crying for dear Zachary. We do miss him so very much. I find myself longing for the sound of that cursed cane of his banging the floor.

Thank you for the letter, and the parcel. You are altogether too generous, dear Elinora. The baby clothes are beautiful and much appreciated. Tell Fanny I shall treasure the shawl she knitted. And the book you sent, Advice To A Mother, has cleared away many of my questions about the birth process. I note that it is written by an Englishwoman; surely the English are more enlightened than the rest of us, to publish so outspoken a volume.

You ask when this blessed event will occur. I see Doctor Witherspoon each time we go to town, and he says about the third week in January. Although I hate the very thought, Noah is adamant that I go and stay with friends in Medicine Hat after Christmas so the doctor will be in attendance at the birth. Elinora, I can't help but feel in my heart that I'm being banished, even though my head tells me the idea is a sensible one. We are far from town, it's winter, and the doctor might not reach us in time.

Enough of my ranting! Truth to tell, I am in perfect health, although I grow to look more like a pumpkin every day. Gladys is quick to inform me that my rounded shape is going to get worse before it gets better. She and Rose came to visit again last week, the first time since the funeral. I think I told you that Zachary is buried in a spot near the river, alongside Noah's first wife and baby. I go there when the weather permits; I feel strangely close to all three of them.

Gladys has become a good friend, and Rose and Bets are as thick as thieves. Rose can sign almost as well as I can. We're planning a get-together for Christmas day. Gladys says her family will come here because of my "condition, "and we'll all make Christmas dinner. Bets and I are busy making gifts—aprons and potpourri from wild roses for the women and socks for the men. I'm making Noah new mittens from scarlet yarn; his are full of holes.

You asked in your letter how Noah is doing with the death of his father, and I have to say I don't really know. You see, he won't talk to me, Elinora. I try, but it's as if he's far away. I did think, just before Zachary's death, that things had changed for the better, but it hasn't worked that way at all.

As always, he is kind and very thoughtful. He brings all the water in and takes the slops out and warns me not to lift heavy things. He bought me two new (voluminous) dresses last trip to town, as nothing I have fits anymore, but he refuses to speak of the baby, which is what I need and want him to do. Every time I've brought it up, he gets up and walks away.

I love him with all my heart, Elinora, and I've come to realize I'm an all-or-nothing sort of person. If he can't see his way to loving me and this child equally, the day will come when I will have to leave.

'Well, this is a sad excuse for a letter, but you told me always to write as I feel. Enclosed is a note from Bets—her penmanship is getting much better, isn't it? I make her do lessons every day. You wouldn't recognize her. She's grown a foot and put on weight and looks a different girl altogether'. Coming here has been good for her, at least.

I hope you are well and not working too hard. Bets and I laughed over your story about the new boarder. I imagine you have her quite house-broken by now.

I hope to hear from you soon. Each time Noah goes to town, I pray for a letter.

Your loving, expectant friend, Annie.

In mid-December, at Bets's urging, Noah cut a bushy willow tree and nailed it to a stand. The sisters decorated its stark branches with strings of cranberries, popcorn, and paper angels.

They tied suet to the outdoor clothesline for the birds and wrapped the gifts they'd made and stacked them under the tree. Noah bought extra sugar in town, and Annie made candy and baked cakes in preparation for Christmas.

The temperature dropped to 38 degrees below zero and stayed there for a week. Annie and Bets fretted over whether it would be too cold for their guests to travel, but on December 23, it suddenly warmed up again, to only 10 below.

All the Christmas preparations were finished, and the house was clean. Annie awoke that morning filled with energy, determined that the time had come to tidy Zachary's bedroom and turn it into a nursery for the baby. She'd been putting it off.

Noah had shut the door to his father's room after the funeral, and it had remained closed. Now, for some reason, it was urgent to her that the room be in order before the next day, when the Hopkins family came over.

She told Noah that morning at breakfast what she was planning, and as usual these days, he didn't really answer her. He simply nodded in. that distracted way he had, pulled on his heavy coat and hat, and disappeared out the door in the direction of the bam.

Half the time, she thought despondently, she didn't know whether he even heard what she said to him.

Annie enlisted Bets's help in dismantling Zachary's bed and setting it against the wall. They folded his clothing neatly into a box, dusted down the walls, and scrubbed the floor. Annie lined the dresser drawers with fresh paper and lovingly laid her meager collection of baby things there, flannel diapers and tiny dresses and knitted leggings that she was certain were too small to fit anything human.

In spite of the freezing temperature, Bets carried the rag rug out to the clothesline and gave it a vigorous beating.

Noah had been out in the barn all morning, shoveling hay down from the loft to load on a sled to take out to the cattle in the south pasture, and when he came in at noon, Annie showed him what they'd done.

"Now we need your help in moving the bed and mattress to the attic," Annie told him, adding with her heart in her throat, "and Noah, do you think you could bring the cradle down?"

All morning, she'd worried over his reaction to that suggestion. She knew Noah had built the cradle before his son was born. Zachary had carved the angels and flowers and wood sprites into the satiny wood, and having it in plain view would be a painful reminder of both dead father and lost child.

The roof in the attic room was too low for him to stand upright. With Bets's help, Noah lowered the awkward mattress to a spot against the wall and, half crouching, forced himself to look around at the things he'd sworn never to look at again, Jeremy's cradle, his high chair, the soft blankets and shawls that had kept him warm, the trunk packed with his baby clothing, the wooden box Noah had fashioned to hold his son's toys.

Bets plucked a stuffed kitten, its tail gone, out of the toy box and stroked it. Then, with a nervous glance at him, she carefully put it back again.

Noah winced, remembering his sturdy, mischievous son pulling on that tail until it finally came loose from the toy.

"Broke," he'd said matter-of-factly, handing it to Noah. "Da fix."

How he missed his little son. How he'd loved him, right from the moment Molly told him she was pregnant. He'd begun the cradle that very day. With pride and delight, he'd watched his wife's body changing, placing his hand on Molly's belly and laughing with awe and joy to feel their child moving. He'd rubbed her back and teased her and laced her boots each morning when she could no longer reach them.

And what had he done for Annie?

Nothing. Nothing at all, except make it plain in every way he could that he didn't want her child. He'd witnessed the anxiety in her eyes just now when she asked him to bring down the cradle.

She'd actually thought he would refuse her even the use of the cradle for the baby she carried.

He straightened suddenly and smacked his head on a rafter. He swore viciously, but the pain mirrored the sudden, shamed anguish in his heart.

He couldn't pretend he wanted this child, because he didn't.

But neither could he deny his feelings for Annie. In spite

of himself, against every vow he'd made, he cared for Annie.

It was for her sake that he lifted the trunk that held Jeremy's baby clothing and carried it downstairs. It was like slowly plucking the scab from a deep, half healed wound, but he returned for the cradle, the box of toys, and the high chair, setting everything in the room that Annie was preparing for the baby.

She watched wide-eyed as he brought down all of Jeremy's things. When he had finished, she came over to him and, without a word, locked her arms around his neck and pulled his head down to kiss him full on the lips.

"Thank you, Noah. I know it's difficult for you, and I thank you." Her green eyes shimmered with tears, and the gratitude and love on her face were more than he could bear.

God, she was beautiful. She'd spilled something brown down her front and she smelled of cooking, and her fiery hair rose like a nimbus around her head, curly and messy and wild, and it came to him that he loved her. He'd loved her for a long time, without being able to admit it to her or to himself.

Longing overwhelmed him, and he wrapped his arms around her and held her close against him, his eyes shut tight, his heart aching for release, imagining for a split second how it might have been with her if only ...

But he could feel the mound of her belly pressing his, and the babe inside suddenly kicked hard against him.

Panic filled Noah at the emotion that contact created.

He jerked away from her embrace and blindly reached for his overcoat and hat. "I'm taking a load of hay out to the cattle this afternoon. I'll be home in time for supper."

His voice was harsh, because something was happening in his chest. A tight knot that he'd never allowed to unwind was stubbornly coming undone.

He fought with all his strength, but the sobs started when

he was halfway across the yard, tearing, painful sobs that he'd denied when Molly was taken from him, when Jeremy died, when he lost his father.

He knew that strong men didn't cry, but he couldn't stop himself any longer. He stumbled into the barn and stood there, arms braced against a stall, tears raining down his face, the savage agony of all his losses bursting in his chest and erupting in an avalanche of grief that he couldn't force down anymore.

At first he fought the tears with all his strength, horrified, ashamed of such weakness, but their power overwhelmed him and at last he gave in, sinking to his knees on the hay and weeping until he was empty.

At last he staggered to his feet, mindful of his cattle needing to be fed. Still in a daze, he harnessed Buck to the loaded sleigh, not taking note that the wind had changed and was now blowing from the north, or that the western sky was bruised looking and inky dark, heavy with storm clouds.

Instead, he looked toward the house. Smoke curled cheerfully from the chimney. It was a dark afternoon, and the lamp shone from the window. He imagined the little Christmas tree and thought he could hear Annie and Bets laughing together as they so often did over their work.

They were his family now, and he desperately wanted to tell them so. He needed the comfort that affirmation would provide, but he couldn't go in now, with red, shamefully swollen eyes. He'd only be gone two hours. He'd tell them when he returned.

When he came home, he'd take Annie in his arms and confess how wrong he'd been all these months. He'd beg her forgiveness, and because he knew her so well by now, he knew she'd give it freely, with all the fervor of her passionate, generous nature.

His chest filled with warmth and anticipation. At the last moment, he remembered the wolves that preyed on his cattle and went back to the barn for his rifle. Then he clucked to Buck and headed off across the snow-covered landscape.

Annie and Bets were totally engrossed by the pleasurable task of readying the baby's room. Bets wiped the cradle down and made it up with its tiny sheets and warm shawls. They smiled and made admiring faces at the wealth of meticulously hand- sewn shirts, knitted sweaters, and tiny flannel nightdresses in the trunk. Annie arranged some of the wooden toys on the dresser, only vaguely aware that the wind had gotten up and snow was beginning to fall outside.

At last Bets drew her attention to the window, and

Annie was shocked at the ferocity of the storm. A flicker of uneasiness made her shiver as she caught sight of the clock.

"Lordie, Bets, we'd better hurry supper. Noah must have come back hours ago. He'll be hungry," she murmured, grunting as she bent over the wood box to get a log for the cook stove. Her huge belly made bending difficult, and her back had been aching on and off all afternoon.

"You peel these potatoes, and I'll start some sausage frying," she instructed her sister. "We'll open a jar of crabapples; they'll do for dessert."

For the next half hour, she and Bets hurried to get the meal prepared, anticipating Noah's arrival at any second. But the minutes passed, and when all was ready and she'd walked to the window a dozen times to peer out, Annie tried to hide her growing concern from Bets.

"Noah must have decided to do the milking early, what with this blizzard," she said. "I'm just going to walk over to the barn and see if I can help. It's getting late."

But Bets grabbed her sister's arm. "You will not. I will go. What if you fall on the ice?" She made a face and a slicing motion across her throat. "Noah will kill me if I let you outside in this." She grabbed an old coat, tied a shawl over her head, and stuck her feet into a pair of Zachary's boots.

Annie went with her to the door. When they opened it, both were shocked at the force of the storm. A maelstrom of wind and snow whirled around Bets as she set off in the direction of the barn.

Annie shut the door and leaned back against it, cupping her hands around her belly, trying to take comfort in the restlessness of the child inside, trying to still the fear that was making her heart hammer and her hands tremble.

Where was Noah?

Chapter Ten

It seemed to Annie that an eternity went by before the kitchen door opened again and Bets was half blown in on a cloud of swirling snow and frigid air. What little daylight there had been was now entirely gone.

Bets tugged off her mitts, but even before her fingers flew with their message, the alarm on her sister's face told Annie what was wrong.

"Noah is not there. He's still gone with Buck and the hay sled."

They stared at one another, their eyes filled with horror.

Outside, the wind howled like a mad demon, and the snow blew thick and blinding. The windowpanes rattled, and even the stoves hissed as snow was driven down the chimney and hit the burning coals.

"Something's happened. Something awful's happened to him, Bets," Annie whispered. Inside her, fear and urgency combined with a terrible feeling of helplessness. A woman big with child, a half-grown girl, a raging blizzard; what in heaven could they do?

"I will ride to Hopkins and get help." Bets's fingers flew.

"I will take Noah's horse, Sultan. I know how to saddle him. Noah showed me."

"Oh, sweetheart, you can't." Annie gave her brave sister a hug, then stood back so she could explain. "For one thing, it's storming far too hard to ride to the Hopkins place. You'd get lost. And for another, Noah's the only one who can ride Sultan. He's a demon, Noah says so himself."

Bets's bravado disappeared and she started to cry. "We must help. We must do something."

Annie reached out and wiped away the tears from her sister's face with a comer of her apron. "We will, but it's not going to help if we go out and get ourselves lost, so we'll wait until the worst of this storm stops and then we'll get on old Bright and go find him together. Bright can carry us both. And in the meantime, we'll light the extra lantern and put it in the window, so if Noah comes, he'll see the light from a distance and not lose his way in the storm."

Even as she signed the optimistic words, Annie knew that blizzards like this could last days and days, and that unless the storm abated soon, it would be too late.

She turned her head and gazed at the frost-covered window. If anything, the wind had increased.

"I love Noah," Bets signed in her forthright manner. "Always, he is good and kind to me. Never he makes me feel less because I am deaf."

Anguish and terror filled Annie's heart, and a low moan came from her throat.

Noah, my husband, where are you?

With all the fierceness of her being, she willed him safe, but she knew that no one could survive long outside in these conditions.

Together, they found the lantern, filled and lit it.

They prepared an emergency bundle with food and dry

clothes and a blanket, and they gathered their warmest clothes, ready to put on at a moment's notice.

But as the night deepened, the storm raged on. Bets finally fell asleep on the couch, but weary as she was, Annie couldn't rest.

She stoked the fires, one hand pressed to her aching back, and walked a million times to the window where the lantern burned, praying each time that the storm had lessened, that some miracle would bring Noah bursting through the door.

It didn't happen. It was a long time later when, half dozing beside Bets, the sudden silence brought Annie fully awake.

The wind had died. She lumbered to her feet and hurried to the window. The lantern, still shining bravely, had kept the pane clear of frost, and outside Annie could see snow falling heavily, but the worst of the blizzard was over. Her eyes flew to the clock.

Four **a.m.** It was Christmas Eve morning, and he'd been gone for more than twelve hours.

She sent up a desperate prayer, then went over and touched Bets.

"It's time to go for Noah," she signed when the girl's eyes opened.

He was within a mile of the cattle when the first of the blizzard hit, and Noah considered turning back, but he knew that if he did, many of his cattle in the south pasture would die; they were already short of feed, and unlike horses, they couldn't paw down to the frozen earth for sustenance.

He'd been allowing Buck to go along at his own speed, but now Noah hollered and used the reins to hurry the big animal onward.

Buck nickered in protest, but he responded, going from an ambling walk to a cumbersome trot. The sleigh where Noah rode atop the hay bounced along, but the wind and snow increased until Noah could hardly make out the horse's shape through the storm.

He drew his scarf up over his nose and mouth, thankful for his buffalo coat but cursing himself for a fool. Being out alone on the prairie in a blizzard was a hazardous thing, and if he'd had his wits about him, he would never have left the ranch.

At last he came upon the huddled shapes of the cattle. Using the pitchfork he'd brought along, Noah unloaded the hay as fast as he could. Driving pellets of snow and the howling wind snatched his breath away, blinding him and making his face and hands numb with cold. The cattle grouped themselves around the feed, backs to the wind.

He should stay here, he knew, waiting out the storm in the dubious protection of the cattle's warm bodies. It was the sensible thing to do, because the trip back would be treacherous.

But who knew how long the blizzard would last? Annie would be terrified at his absence, and she was close to her birthing time.

He needed to tell her how much he wanted their baby. ... .

He had to get home, even though by now he couldn't see a single foot in front of him, and all his usual good sense of direction was gone.

Buck would know where the ranch was. Animals were uncanny in that regard.

Swiftly undoing the harness, Noah abandoned the sleigh.

"Let's go home, old man." Rifle on his shoulder, Noah leaped up to the horse's broad back, noting that already there was no sign of the tracks they'd made; the blowing snow had obliterated everything.

The horse stood for a moment, getting his bearings, then

began to move steadily ahead into what seemed a holocaust.

Time disappeared in the unholy force of the storm. Noah, lying almost flat along Buck's broad back, had no idea how long they'd been blundering through the knee-deep drifts when suddenly the big horse stumbled and Noah heard the horrifying crack of breaking bone and, in the next instant, his horse's awful scream of agony as Buck's broken foreleg crumpled beneath him.

Knowing he was in danger of being pinned beneath the huge animal's body, Noah tried to throw himself free.

He landed on a patch of frozen ground blown free of snow, and the impact stunned him, but he could hear Buck's unendurable screaming even over the roaring of the wind. It sickened him.

He knew what he had to do as he scrambled to his feet and searched frantically for his rifle. Finding it, he struggled against the might of the storm to reach Buck, nausea choking him.

"Easy, old friend, my poor old friend."

He cursed in a long, helpless stream. Then he tugged off his mittens, raised the rifle, laid it against Buck's head, and pulled the trigger.

The screaming stopped, and Noah retched into the snow. It was only when the sickness passed and reason returned that he was able to acknowledge that the animal's death almost certainly meant his own.

Already, his fingers were numb, his toes aching with the cold. He crouched beside the still-warm carcass, his mind as chaotic as the storm that raged around him, and what he thought of first was Annie.

If he died here, he'd never have the chance to tell her that he loved her. He'd never see the baby they'd made together. He wouldn't be around to make sure that the young men who came courting pretty Bets in a year or two were suitable.

Damnation, if he died, there'd soon be suitors lining up and fighting over Annie.

She was full of life, passionate, funny, endearing. In fact, Noah admitted, Annie was everything any man could ever want in a wife. And confound it, she *was his.*

The thought of those faceless men daring to come courting his wife sent a rush of jealousy and primitive anger through Noah, and with the anger came determination.

He wasn't going to die out here, damn it. There'd been enough tragedy in the Ferguson family. He refused to add to it.

He needed the chance to set things right, to tell Annie he loved her, to welcome his new son or daughter, to live out the rest of the years of his life unafraid of what fate might bring. He'd been a total fool this past year, but he was going to make up for it.

Like a light going on in the depths of his soul, Noah knew he was going to survive. He just had to figure out how.

His mind became very focused, very clear.

Setting off on foot in this howling storm would certainly get him lost. He'd wander in circles and finally freeze to death.

He had to stay where he was. His only chance lay in the hope that the storm would blow itself out before Buck's huge carcass began to grow cold. If the wind finally died, Noah knew that his sense of direction would unerringly tell him which way to go, but in the meantime, his only chance was to huddle close to the dead horse, using him as a shield against the storm.

With the image of Annie and all the things he had to say to her firmly lodged in his brain, Noah hunkered down beside Buck and waited, pressing himself against the still warm horseflesh.

At last the wind lessened. It was still black dark and

snowing when he stood up. There was no guarantee that the storm was really over, but he was cold and dangerously sleepy.

Sending a silent thanks and a last good-bye to the old horse, Noah stamped feet that felt like blocks of solid ice and staggered off across the snow covered landscape in the direction he prayed would lead him to the ranch.

Chapter Eleven

Annie and Bets gave the old workhorse his head, and Bright stoically waded through the drifts with the two of them perched on him.

Every few moments, Annie called Noah's name, but the sound was muffled by the heavy fall of snow. Her hands and feet grew numb with cold, and she was grateful for Bets's warm body pressing close against her aching back.

Her throat was hoarse from hollering when at last she thought she heard an answer, faint and far away.

"Whoa." She tugged on Bright's reins, afraid even to hope.

"Noah?" Her voice sounded lost in the icy darkness.

"Noooaah," she screamed, every ounce of her own desperation in the call, and this time she was certain she heard his voice respond.

She urged Bright on, and soon a tall, snow covered figure came staggering out of the darkness toward them.

"Noah." With a mixture of laughter and tears, Annie slid down from Bright's back and into his half frozen arms.

"Oh, Noah, thank God you're all right. What happened? Where's Buck?"

In a few stark sentences, he told her, holding her close, his strong arms locked like a vise around her, her huge belly cradled against him.

"I've been such a damned fool, Annie," he said in a hoarse whisper. "I love you, and I'll love this baby of ours when it comes. Now, let's hurry and get you home where it's warm. It's Christmas Eve, and we're going to celebrate, just the three of us."

She turned her face up to him, green eyes full of joyful wonder, hardly able to believe what she'd heard. And in that ecstatic moment, the first horrendous pain ripped through her abdomen.

"Owwww!"

Holding her, Noah felt her brace with the contraction, then fall against him, stunned at its intensity and duration.

A new and awful fear gripped him. He supported her until it was over, doing his best not to let her suspect the utter panic that he felt.

Was she about to have their baby in the middle of this snowstorm? He kept his voice calm so as not to alarm her.

"How long have you been having pains, Annie?"

She leaned on him, panting as the pain receded, her forehead damp with perspiration and snowflakes. "Only this one, but my back's been sore all day."

Noah swallowed hard. God willing, there'd be time to get her home, but the baby was undoubtedly coming, and the storm would make it impossible to bring the doctor. Even sending Bets for Gladys Hopkins was out of the question. It was too far and there was far too much snow.

He'd birthed animals, plenty of them, but Noah hadn't even been allowed in the room when Jeremy was born.

"Let's get you home, sweetheart." Catching Annie under the arms, he lifted her up on Bright's back. "We'll be there in a few minutes." He pulled a frozen mitten off and with a few rapid signs, told Bets what was happening.

"Hold her tight, Bets," he signed.

A few moments before, struggling exhausted and alone through the darkness and the snow, Noah had thought with every single step that he couldn't force himself to take another.

Now, he took Bright's reins and ran easily beside the huge horse. They had to stop twice more as sharp pains gripped Annie, and giddy relief spilled through Noah when at last the lantern the women had lighted and left in the window became visible in the distance, shining through the snow, a beacon welcoming Noah and his family home.

Later, Annie remembered the haze of the lamplight as Noah gripped her hands in his strong ones and urged her to push out their child.

His sleeves were rolled up, and perspiration rolled down his face. He smiled and spoke loving words of encouragement, giving her not the slightest inkling that he was deathly afraid that he'd be unequal to the task ahead of him.

As soon as they had Annie warm and settled, Bets had brought him the book Elinora had sent, entitled *Advice To A Mother.*

Desperate for any small bit of assistance, Noah flipped through it. The book actually had illustrations that depicted the birth of a child, and he propped it on the bedroom dresser and dragged the dresser close to the bed. Referring to the instructions it contained, he and Bets lit lamps and found scissors and folded flannel into pads and filled the copper washtubs with water and set them to heating.

With Bets in charge of keeping the fires burning well and fetching anything he thought he needed, Noah stationed himself beside Annie, glancing more and more distractedly at the book as the hours passed, urging Bets to turn the pages back and forth, soundly cursing the volume's numerous omissions as the birth inevitably progressed in spite of him.

* * *

At ten past noon on December 24, 1886, with the able assistance of his young sister-in-law, Noah Ferguson successfully delivered his tiny daughter, Mary Elinora.

Annie and Bets survived the ordeal exceptionally well, but the first sound of his baby's outraged squalling so relieved her father that dizziness overcame him, and he had to sink down on the bed with her minute, naked body cradled awkwardly in his two huge hands.

He actually thought for the first time in his life that he was about to faint, and he had to draw deep breaths before he could really examine the child he held.

She was scrawny, but already he could sense Mary's enormous life force. The damp curls plastered against her minute skull were undeniably red, and when she opened her eyes and looked vaguely up at him, Noah saw an exact reflection of his own coal-dark gaze.

Annie was watching, and it was evident from the besotted expression on his face that in that first instant, Mary Elinora had captured her father's mighty heart in her tiny fist.

Annie and Bets looked at each other with tears in their eyes and giggled.

From their vantage point in a corner of the room, an old man and a young woman with a laughing little boy between them smiled angelic smiles and nodded at one another with the satisfaction of a job well done. They alone could clearly see the magnificent golden glow that filled the room, the radiance of intense and lasting love, and at last they knew it was time for them, too, to leave, to go toward the light.

ABOUT THE AUTHOR

Bobby Hutchinson was born in a small town in interior British Columbia in 1940. Her father was an underground coal miner, her mother a housewife, and both were storytellers. Learning to read was the most significant event in her early life.

She married young and had three sons. Her middle son was deaf, and he taught her patience. She divorced and worked at various odd jobs, directing traffic around construction sites, day caring challenged children, selling fabric by the pound at a remnant store.

She mortgaged her house and bought the store, took her sewing machine to work, and began to sew a dress a day. The dresses sold. The fabric didn't, so she hired four seamstresses and turned the store into a handmade clothing boutique.

After twelve successful years, she sold the business and decided to run a marathon. Training was a huge bore, so she made up a story as she ran, about Pheiddipedes, the first marathoner. She copied it down and sent it to the Chatelaine short story contest, won first prize, finished the Vancouver marathon, and became a writer. It was a hell of a lot easier than running.

She married again and divorced again, writing all the while, mostly romances, (which she obviously needs to learn a lot about,) and now has more than fifty-five published books.

She decided she needed something to do in the morning in her spare time, so she opened her first B&B, Blue Collar, in Vancouver, B.C. After five successful years, she moved home to the small coal mining town of Sparwood, where she now operates the reincarnated version of the Blue Collar.

She's currently working on three or four or eight more books. She has six enchanting grandchildren. She lives alone, apart from guests, meditates, bikes, reads incessantly, and writes.

She likes a quote by Dolly Parton: "Decide who you are, and then do it on purpose."

Bobby loves to connect with her readers. Visit her online at her:

http://bobbyhutchinson.ca/
http://www.facebook.com/BobbyHutchinsonBooks
https://twitter.com/bluecollarbobby

More Books By Bobby Hutchinson

MEMOIRS:
HOW NOT TO RUN A B&B
TILL DISEASE DO US PART (MEMOIR)

KID'S BOOK:
DEETER, THE DOG WHO DIDN'T LISTEN

MEDICAL ROMANCES

PATIENT CARE
DRASTIC MEASURES
DOUBLE JEOPARDY
ARE YOU MY DADDY?
PICKING CLOVER
FULL RECOVERY
THE BABY DOCTOR
NURSING THE DOCTOR
DRASTIC MEASURES

LANTERN IN THE WINDOW (HISTORICAL ROMANCE)

ANGEL BOOKS:

EARTH ANGEL
ALMOST AN ANGEL

SINGLES

GRADY'S KIDS (WESTERN ROMANCE)
A LEGAL AFFAIR
FOLLOW A WILD HEART

Made in the USA
San Bernardino, CA
17 March 2014